S0-AFJ-673

She hardly noticed when Sam carried her through the main room and dropped her onto her bed.

In a few short seconds, they were both naked. The quilt felt cool beneath her, but he was there, sliding on top of her, to bring the heat.

"Been wanting to peel you out of those sweaters for days now," he murmured, trailing kisses from her belly to her breasts.

"Been wanting you to do it," Joy assured him, and ran the flat of her hands over his shoulders.

She hadn't felt this way in...ever. He shifted, kissing her mouth, tangling his tongue with hers. She lifted her hips into his touch and held his head to hers as they kissed, as they took and gave and then did it all again. Their breath mingled, their hearts pounded in a wild tandem that raced faster and faster as they tasted, explored, discovered.

It was like being caught in a hurricane.

There was no safe place to hide, even if she wanted to. And she didn't. She wanted the storm, more than she'd ever wanted anything in her life.

Dear Reader,

I love Christmas books—reading them *and* writing them. This time of year, I buy every holiday-themed book I can and treat myself to a romance marathon. So when the idea for *Maid Under the Mistletoe* popped into my head, I couldn't have been more pleased.

Sam Henry is a world-famous painter whose world crashed down around him a few years ago. In response to the tragedy, he's turned his back on what he loves most—his work and his family.

Joy Curran is a woman who always sees the bright side of any given situation. She's the mother of Holly, a precocious five-year-old girl who, like her mother, naturally assumes that everyone loves Christmas as much as they do.

When these three people come together, it's an eye-opener for Sam and a lesson in patience for Joy.

I really do love this book and had so much fun writing it. I hope you love it, too—and in this holiday season, I wish you much joy, whichever holiday you're celebrating!

Happy reading!

Maureen Child

MAUREEN CHILD

—————

MAID UNDER THE MISTLETOE

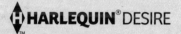

If you purchased this book without a cover you should be aware
that this book is stolen property. It was reported as "unsold and
destroyed" to the publisher, and neither the author nor the
publisher has received any payment for this "stripped book."

Recycling programs
for this product may
not exist in your area.

ISBN-13: 978-0-373-73500-6

Maid Under the Mistletoe

Copyright © 2016 by Maureen Child

All rights reserved. Except for use in any review, the reproduction or
utilization of this work in whole or in part in any form by any electronic,
mechanical or other means, now known or hereinafter invented, including
xerography, photocopying and recording, or in any information storage
or retrieval system, is forbidden without the written permission of the
publisher, Harlequin Enterprises Limited, 225 Duncan Mill Road,
Don Mills, Ontario M3B 3K9, Canada.

This is a work of fiction. Names, characters, places and incidents are
either the product of the author's imagination or are used fictitiously,
and any resemblance to actual persons, living or dead, business
establishments, events or locales is entirely coincidental.

This edition published by arrangement with Harlequin Books S.A.

For questions and comments about the quality of this book,
please contact us at CustomerService@Harlequin.com.

® and TM are trademarks of Harlequin Enterprises Limited or its
corporate affiliates. Trademarks indicated with ® are registered in the
United States Patent and Trademark Office, the Canadian Intellectual
Property Office and in other countries.

Printed in U.S.A.

www.Harlequin.com

Maureen Child writes for the Harlequin Desire line and can't imagine a better job. A seven-time finalist for a prestigious Romance Writers of America RITA® Award, Maureen is an author of more than one hundred romance novels. Her books regularly appear on bestseller lists and have won several awards, including a Prism Award, a National Readers' Choice Award, a Colorado Romance Writers Award of Excellence and a Golden Quill Award. She is a native Californian but has recently moved to the mountains of Utah.

Books by Maureen Child

Harlequin Desire

The Fiancée Caper
After Hours with Her Ex
Triple the Fun
Double the Trouble
The Baby Inheritance
Maid Under the Mistletoe

Pregnant by the Boss

Having Her Boss's Baby
A Baby for the Boss
Snowbound with the Boss

Visit her Author Profile page at Harlequin.com, or maureenchild.com, for more titles.

To all the moms who are out there
right now, making magic

One

Sam Henry hated December.

The days were too short, making the nights seem an eternity. It was cold and dark—and then there was the incessant Christmas badgering. Lights, trees, carols and an ever-increasing barrage of commercials urging you to shop, spend, buy. And every reminder of the holiday season ate at the edges of his soul and heart like drops of acid.

He scowled at the roaring fire in the hearth, slapped one hand on the mantel and rubbed his fingers over the polished edge of the wood. With his gaze locked on the flames, he told himself that if he could, he'd wipe the month of December from the calendar.

"You can't stick your head in the snow and pretend Christmas isn't happening."

Sam flicked a glance at the woman in the open doorway. His housekeeper/cook/nag, Kaye Porter, stood there glaring at him through narrowed blue eyes. Hands at her wide hips, her gray-streaked black hair pulled back into a single thick braid that hung down over one shoulder, she shook her head. "There's not enough snow to do it anyway, and whether you like it or not, Christmas is coming."

"I don't and it's only coming if I acknowledge it," Sam told her.

"Well, you're going to have to pay attention because I'm out of here tomorrow."

"I'll give you a raise if you cancel your trip," he said, willing to bargain to avoid the hassle of losing the woman who ran his house so he didn't have to.

A short bark of laughter shot from her throat. "Not a chance. My friend Ruthie and I do this every year, as you well know. We've got our rooms booked and there's no way we're canceling."

He'd known that—he just hadn't wanted to think about it. Another reason to hate December. Every year, Kaye and Ruthie took a month-long vacation. A cruise to the Bahamas, then a stay at a splashy beachside hotel, followed by another cruise home. Kaye liked to say it was her therapy to get her through the rest of the year living with a crank like himself.

"If you love Christmas so much, why do you run to a beach every year?"

She sighed heavily. "Christmas is everywhere, you know. Even in hot, sandy places! We buy little trees, decorate them for our rooms. And the hotel lights up all the palm trees…" She sighed again, but this time, it was with delight. "It's gorgeous."

"Fine." He pushed away from the hearth, tucked both hands into the pockets of his jeans and stared at her. Every year he tried to talk her out of leaving and every year he lost. Surrendering to the inevitable, he asked, "You need a ride to the airport?"

A small smile curved her mouth at the offer. "No, but thanks. Ruthie's going to pick me up at the crack of dawn tomorrow. She'll leave her car there so when we come back we don't have to worry about taking one of those damn shuttles."

"Okay then." He took a breath and muttered, "Have a great time."

"The enthusiasm in that suggestion is just one of the reasons I need this trip." One dark eyebrow lifted. "You worry me, Sam. All locked away on this mountain hardly talking to anyone but me—"

She kept going, but Sam tuned out. He'd heard it all before. Kaye was determined to see him "start living" again. Didn't seem to matter that he had no interest in that. While she talked, he glanced around the main room of what Kaye liked to call his personal prison.

It was a log home, the wood the color of warm honey, with lots of glass to spotlight the view that was breathtaking from every room. Pine forest surrounded the house, and a wide, private lake stretched out beyond a narrow slice of beach. He had a huge garage and several outbuildings, including a custom-designed workshop where Sam wished he was right at that moment.

This house, this *sanctuary*, was just what he'd been looking for when he'd come to Idaho five years ago. It was isolated, with a small town—Franklin—just fifteen minutes away when he needed supplies. A big city, with the airport and all manner of other distractions, was just an hour from there, not that he ever went. What he needed, he had Kaye pick up in Franklin and only rarely went to town himself.

The whole point of moving here had been to find quiet. Peace. *Solitude*. Hell, he could go weeks and never talk to anyone but Kaye. Thoughts of her brought him back to the conversation at hand.

"…Anyway," she was saying, "my friend Joy will be here about ten tomorrow morning to fill in for me while I'm gone."

He nodded. At least Kaye had done what she always did, arranged for one of her friends to come and stay for the month she'd be gone. Sam wouldn't have to worry about cooking, cleaning or pretty much anything but keeping his distance from whatever busy-body she'd found this year.

He folded his arms over his chest. "I'm not going to catch this one rifling through my desk, right?"

Kaye winced. "I will admit that having Betty come last year was a bad idea…"

"Yeah," he agreed. She'd seemed nice enough, but the woman had poked her head into everything she could find. Within a week, Sam had sent her home and had spent the following three weeks eating grilled cheese sandwiches, canned soup and frozen pizza. "I'd say so."

"She's the curious sort."

"She's nosy."

"Yes, well." Kaye cleared her throat. "That was my mistake, I know. But my friend Joy isn't a snoop. I think you'll like her."

"Not necessary," he assured her. He didn't want to like Joy. Hell, he didn't want to *talk* to her if he could avoid it.

"Of course not." Kaye shook her head again and gave him the kind of look teachers used to reserve for the kid acting up in class. "Wouldn't want to be human or anything. Might set a nasty precedent."

"Kaye…"

The woman had worked for him since he'd moved to Idaho five years ago. And since then, she'd muscled her way much deeper into his life than he'd planned on allowing. Not only did she take care of the house, but she looked after *him* despite the fact that he didn't want her to. But Kaye was a force of nature, and it seemed her friends were a lot like her.

"Never mind. Anyway, to what I was saying, Joy already knows that you're cranky and want to be left alone—"

He frowned at her. "Thanks."

"Am I wrong?" When he didn't answer, she nodded. "She's a good cook and runs her own business on the internet."

"You told me all of this already," he pointed out. Though she hadn't said what *kind* of business the amazing Joy ran. Still, how many different things could a woman in her fifties or sixties do online? Give knitting lessons? Run a babysitting service? Dog sitting? Hell, his own mother sold handmade dresses online, so there was just no telling.

"I know, I know." Kaye waved away his interruption. "She'll stay out of your way because she needs this time here. The contractor says they won't have the fire damage at her house repaired until January, so being able to stay and work here was a godsend."

"You told me this, too," he reminded her. In fact, he'd heard more than enough about Joy the Wonder Friend. According to Kaye, she was smart, clever, a hard worker, had a wonderful sense of humor and did apparently everything just short of walking on water. "But how did the fire in her house start again?

Is she a closet arsonist? A terrible cook who set fire to the stove?"

"Of course not!" Kaye sniffed audibly and stiffened as if someone had shoved a pole down the back of her sweatshirt. "I told you, there was a short in the wiring. The house she's renting is just ancient and something was bound to go at some point. The owner of the house is having all the wiring redone, though, so it should be safe now."

"I'm relieved to hear it," he said. And relieved he didn't have to worry that Kaye's friend was so old she'd forgotten to turn off an oven or something.

"I'm only trying to tell you—" she broke off to give him a small smile of understanding "—like I do every year, that you'll survive the month of December just like you do every year."

He ground his teeth together at the flash of sympathy that stirred and then vanished from her eyes. This was the problem with people getting to know too much about him. They felt as if they had the right to offer comfort where none was wanted—or needed. Sam liked Kaye fine, but there were parts of his life that were closed off. For a reason.

He'd get through the holidays his way. Which meant ignoring the forced cheer and the never-ending lineup of "feel good" holiday-themed movies where the hard-hearted hero does a turnaround and opens himself to love and the spirit of Christmas.

Hearts should never be open. Left them too vulnerable to being shattered.

And he'd never set himself up for that kind of pain again.

Early the following day Kaye was off on her vacation, and a few hours later Sam was swamped by the empty silence. He reminded himself that it was how he liked his life best. No one bothering him. No one talking at him. One of the reasons he and Kaye got along so well was that she respected his need to be left the hell alone. So now that he was by himself in the big house, why did he feel an itch along his spine?

"It's December," he muttered aloud. That was enough to explain the sense of discomfort that clung to him.

Hell, every year, this one damn month made life damn near unlivable. He pushed a hand through his hair, then scraped that hand across the stubble on his jaw. He couldn't settle. Hadn't even spent any time out in his workshop, and usually being out there eased his mind and kept him too busy to think about—

He put the brakes on that thought fast because he couldn't risk opening doors that were better off sealed shut.

Scowling, he stared out the front window at the cold, dark day. The steel-gray clouds hung low enough that it looked as though they were actually skimming across the tops of the pines. The lake, in summer a brilliant sapphire blue, stretched out in front of him like a sheet of frozen pewter. The whole damn world seemed bleak and bitter, which only fed into what he felt every damn minute.

Memories rose up in the back of his mind, but he squelched them flat, as he always did. He'd worked too hard for too damn long to get beyond his past, to live and breathe—and hell, *survive*—to lose it all now. He'd beaten back his demons, and damned if he'd release them long enough to take a bite out of him now.

Resolve set firmly, Sam frowned again when an old blue four-door sedan barreled along his drive, kicking up gravel as it came to a stop in front of the house. For a second, he thought it must be Kaye's friend Joy arriving. Then the driver stepped out of the car and that thought went out the window.

The driver was too young, for one thing. Every other friend Kaye had enlisted to help out had been her age or older. This woman was in her late twenties, he figured, gaze locked on her as she turned her face to stare up at the house. One look at her and Sam felt a punch of lust that stole his breath. Everything in him fisted tightly as he continued to watch her. He couldn't take his eyes off her as she stood on the drive studying his house. Hell, she was like a ray of sunlight in the gray.

Her short curly hair was bright blond and flew about her face in the sharp wind that slapped rosy color into her cheeks. Her blue eyes swept the exterior of the house even as she moved around the car to the rear passenger side. Her black jeans hugged long legs, and her hiking boots looked scarred and well-worn. The cardinal-red parka she wore over a cream-colored sweater was a burst of color in a black-and-white world.

She was beautiful and moved with a kind of easy grace that made a man's gaze follow her every movement. And even while he admitted that silently, Sam resented it. He wasn't interested in women. Didn't want to feel what she was making him feel. What he had to do was find out why the hell she was there and get her gone as fast as possible.

She had to be lost. His drive wasn't that easy to find—purposely. He rarely got visitors, and those were mainly his family when he couldn't stave off his parents or sister any longer.

Well, if she'd lost her way, he'd go out and give her directions to town, and then she'd be gone and he could get back to—whatever.

"Damn." The single word slipped from his throat as she opened the car's back door and a little girl jumped out. The eager anticipation stamped on the child's face was like a dagger to the heart for Sam. He took a breath that fought its way into his chest and forced himself to look away from the kid. He didn't do kids. Not for a long time now. Their voices. Their laughter. They were too small. Too vulnerable.

Too breakable.

What felt like darkness opened up in the center of his chest. Turning his back on the window, he left the room and headed for the front door. The faster he got rid of the gorgeous woman and her child, the better.

"It's a fairy castle, Mommy!"

Joy Curran glanced at the rearview mirror and smiled at the excitement shining on her daughter's face. At five years old, Holly was crazy about princesses, fairies and everyday magic she seemed to find wherever she looked.

Still smiling, Joy shifted her gaze from her daughter to the big house in front of her. Through the windshield, she scanned the front of the place and had to agree with Holly on this one. It did look like a castle.

Two stories, it spread across the land, pine trees spearing up all around it like sentries prepared to stand in defense. The smooth, glassy logs were the color of warm honey, and the wide, tall windows gave glimpses of the interior. A wraparound porch held chairs and gliders that invited visitors to sit and get comfortable. The house faced a private lake where a long dock jutted out into the water that was frozen over for winter. There was a wide deck studded with furniture draped in tarps for winter and a brick fire pit.

It would probably take her a half hour to look at everything, and it was way too cold to simply sit

in her car and take it all in. So instead, she turned
the engine off, then walked around to get Holly out
of her car seat. While the little girl jumped up and
down in excitement, pigtails flying, Joy grabbed
her purse and headed for the front door. The cold
wrapped itself around them and Joy shivered. There
hadn't been much snow so far this winter, but the
cold sliced right down to the bone. All around her,
the pines were green but the grass was brown, dotted with shrinking patches of snow. Holly kept hoping to make snow angels and snowmen, but so far,
Mother Nature wasn't cooperating.

The palatial house looked as if it had grown right
out of the woods surrounding it. The place was gorgeous, but a little intimidating. And from everything
she'd heard, so was the man who lived here. Oh, Kaye
was crazy about him, but then Kaye took in stray
dogs, cats, wounded birds and any lonely soul she
happened across. But there was plenty of speculation
about Sam Henry in town.

Joy knew he used to be a painter, and she'd actually seen a few of his paintings online. Judging by
the art he created, she would have guessed him to be
warm, optimistic and, well, *nice*. According to Kaye,
though, the man was quiet, reclusive to the point of
being a hermit, and she thought he was lonely at the
bottom of it. But to Joy's way of thinking, if you
didn't want to be lonely, you got out and met people. Heck, it was so rare to see Sam Henry in town,

spotting him was the equivalent of a Bigfoot sighting. She'd caught only the occasional rare glimpse of the man herself.

But none of that mattered at the moment, Joy told herself. She and Holly needed a place to stay for the month, and this housesitting/cooking/cleaning job had turned up at just the right time. Taking Holly's hand, she headed for the front door, the little girl skipping alongside her, chattering about princesses and castles the whole way.

For just a second, Joy envied her little girl's simpler outlook on life. For Holly, this was an adventure in a magical castle. For Joy, it was moving into a big, secluded house with a secretive and, according to Kaye, cranky man. Okay, now she was making it sound like she was living in a Gothic novel. Kaye lived here year-round, right? And had for years. Surely Joy could survive a month. Determined now to get off on the right foot, she plastered a smile on her face, climbed up to the wide front porch and knocked on the double doors.

She was still smiling a moment later when the door was thrown open and she looked up into a pair of suspicious brown eyes. An instant snap of attraction slapped at Joy, surprising her with its force. His black hair was long, hitting past the collar of his dark red shirt, and the thick mass lifted slightly as another cold wind trickled past. His jaws were shadowed by whiskers and his mouth was a grim straight line.

He was tall, with broad shoulders, narrow hips and long legs currently encased in worn, faded denim that stacked on the tops of a pair of weathered brown cowboy boots.

If it wasn't for the narrowed eyes and the grim expression on his face, he would have been the star of any number of Joy's personal fantasies. Then he spoke and the already tattered remnants of said fantasy drifted away.

"This is private property," he said in a voice that was more of a growl. "If you're looking for town, go back to the main road and turn left. Stay on the road and you'll get there in about twenty minutes."

Well, this was starting off well.

"Thanks," she said, desperately trying to hang on to the smile curving her mouth as well as her optimistic attitude. "But I'm not lost. I've just come from town."

If anything, his frown deepened. "Then why're you here?"

"Nice to meet you, too," Joy said, half tugging Holly behind her. Not that she was afraid of him—but why subject her little girl to a man who looked like he'd rather slam the door in their faces than let them in?

"I repeat," he said, "who are you?"

"I'm Joy. Kaye's friend?" It came out as a question though she hadn't meant it as one.

"You're kidding." His eyes went wide as his gaze

swept her up and down in a fast yet thorough examination.

She didn't know whether to be flattered or insulted. But when his features remained stiff and cold, she went for insulted.

"Is there a problem?" she asked. "Kaye told me you'd be expecting me and—"

"You're not old."

She blinked at him. "Thank you for noticing, though I've got to say, if Kaye ever hears you call her 'old,' it won't be pretty."

"That's not—" He stopped and started again. "I was expecting a woman Kaye's age," he continued. "Not someone like you. Or," he added with a brief glance at Holly, "a child."

Why hadn't Kaye told him about Holly? For a split second, Joy worried over that and wondered if he'd try to back out of their deal now. But an instant later she assured herself that no matter what happened, she was going to hold him to his word. She needed to be here and she wasn't about to leave.

She took a breath and ignored the cool chill in his eyes. "Well, that's a lovely welcome, thanks. Look, it's cold out here. If you don't mind, I'd like to come in and get settled."

He shook his head, opened his mouth to speak, but Holly cut him off.

"Are you the prince?" She stepped out from behind her mother, tipped her head back and studied him.

"The what?"

Joy tensed. She didn't want to stop Holly from talking—wasn't entirely sure she *could*—but she was more than willing to intervene if the quietly hostile man said something she didn't like.

"The prince," Holly repeated, the tiny lisp that defined her voice tugging at Joy's heart. "Princes live in castles."

Joy caught the barest glimmer of a smile brush across his face before it was gone again. Somehow, though, that ghost of real emotion made her feel better.

"No," he said and his voice was softer than it had been. "I'm not a prince."

Joy could have said something to that, and judging by the glance he shot her, he half expected her to. But irritating him further wasn't going to get her and Holly into the house and out of the cold.

"But he looks like a prince, doesn't he, Mommy?"

A prince with a lousy attitude. A dark prince, maybe.

"Sure, honey," she said with a smile for the little girl shifting from foot to foot in her eagerness to get inside the "castle."

Turning back to the man who still stood like an immovable object in the doorway, Joy said reasonably, "Look, I'm sorry we aren't what you were expecting. But here we are. Kaye told you about the fire at our house, right?"

"The firemen came and let me sit in the big truck with the lights going and it was really bright and blinking."

"Is that right?" That vanishing smile of his came and went again in a blink.

"And it smelled really bad," Holly put in, tugging her hand free so she could pinch her own nose.

"It did," Joy agreed, running one hand over the back of Holly's head. "And," she continued, "it did enough damage that we can't stay there while they're fixing it—" She broke off and said, "Can we finish this inside? It's cold out here."

For a second, she wasn't sure he'd agree, but then he nodded, moved back and opened the wide, heavy door. Heat rushed forward to greet them, and Joy nearly sighed in pleasure. She gave a quick look around at the entry hall. The gleaming, honey-colored logs shone in the overhead light. The entry floor was made up of huge square tiles in mottled earth tones. Probably way easier to clean up melting snow from tile floors instead of wood, she told herself and let her gaze quickly move over what she could see of the rest of the house.

It seemed even bigger on the inside, which was hard to believe, and with the lights on against the dark of winter, the whole place practically glowed. A long hallway led off to the back of the house, and on the right was a stairway leading to the second floor. Near the front door, there was a handmade coat tree boasting a half-dozen brass hooks and a padded bench attached.

Shrugging out of her parka, Joy hung it on one of the hooks, then turned and pulled Holly's jacket off as well, hanging it alongside hers. The warmth of the house surrounded her and all Joy could think was, she really wanted to stay. She and Holly needed a place and this house with its soft glow was...welcoming, in spite of its owner.

She glanced at the man watching her, and one look told her that he really wanted her gone. But she wasn't going to allow that.

The house was gigantic, plenty of room for her and Holly to live and still stay out of Sam Henry's way. There was enough land around the house so that her little girl could play. One man to cook and clean for, which would leave her plenty of time to work on her laptop. And oh, if he made them leave, she and her daughter would end up staying in a hotel in town for a month. Just the thought of trying to keep a five-year-old happy when she was trapped in a small, single room for weeks made Joy tired.

"Okay, we're inside," he said. "Let's talk."

"Right. It's a beautiful house." She walked past him, forcing the man to follow her as she walked to the first doorway and peeked in. A great room—that really lived up to the name.

Floor-to-ceiling windows provided a sweeping view of the frozen lake, a wide lawn and a battalion of pines that looked to be scraping the underside of the low-hanging gray clouds. There was a massive hearth on one wall, where a wood fire burned merrily. A big-screen TV took up most of another wall, and there were brown leather couches and chairs sprinkled around the room, sitting on brightly colored area rugs. Handcrafted wood tables held lamps and books, with more books tucked onto shelves lining yet another wall.

"I love reading, too, and what a terrific spot for it," Joy said, watching Holly as the girl wandered the room, then headed straight to the windows where she peered out, both hands flat against the glass.

"Yeah, it works for me." He came up beside her, crossed his arms over his chest and said, "Anyway..."

"You won't even know we're here," Joy spoke up quickly. "And it'll be a pleasure to take care of this place. Kaye loves working here, so I'm sure Holly and I will be just as happy."

"Yeah, but—"

She ignored his frown and the interruption. On a roll, she had no intention of stopping. "I'm going to take a look around. You don't have to worry about giving me a tour. I'll find my own way—"

"About that—"

Irritation flashed across his features and Joy almost felt sorry for him. Not sorry enough to stop, though. "What time do you want dinner tonight?"

Before he could answer, she said, "How about six?

If that works for you, we'll keep it that way for the month. Otherwise, we can change it."

"I didn't agree—"

"Kaye said Holly and I should use her suite of rooms off the kitchen, so we'll just go get settled in and you can get back to what you were doing when we got here." A bright smile on her face, she called, "Holly, come with me now." She looked at him. "Once I've got our things put away, I'll look through your supplies and get dinner started, if it's all right with you." *And even if it isn't*, she added silently.

"Talking too fast to be interrupted doesn't mean this is settled," he told her flatly.

The grim slash of his mouth matched the iciness in his tone. But Joy wasn't going to give up easily. "There's nothing to settle. We agreed to be here for the month and that's what we're going to do."

He shook his head. "I don't think this is going to work out."

"You can't know that, and I think you're wrong," she said, stiffening her spine as she faced him down. She needed this job. This place. For one month. And she wouldn't let him take it from her. Keeping her voice low so Holly wouldn't overhear, she said, "I'm holding you to the deal we made."

"*We* didn't make a deal."

"You did with Kaye."

"Kaye's not here."

"Which is why we are." *One point to me.* Joy

grinned and met his gaze, deliberately glaring right into those shuttered brown eyes of his.

"Are there fairies in the woods?" Holly wondered aloud.

"I don't know, honey," Joy said.

"No," Sam told her.

Holly's face fell and Joy gave him a stony glare. He could be as nasty and unfriendly with her as he wanted to be. But he wouldn't be mean to her daughter. "He means he's never seen any fairies, sweetie."

"Oh." The little girl's smile lit up her face. "Me either. But maybe I can sometime, Mommy says."

With a single look, Joy silently dared the man to pop her daughter's balloon again. But he didn't.

"Then you'll have to look harder, won't you?" he said instead, then lifted his gaze to Joy's. With what looked like regret glittering in his eyes, he added, "You'll have a whole month to look for them."

Two

A few hours in the workshop didn't improve Sam's mood. Not a big surprise. How the hell could he clear his mind when it was full of images of Joy Curran and her daughter?

As her name floated through his mind *again*, Sam deliberately pushed it away, though he knew damn well she'd be sliding back in. Slowly, methodically, he ran the hand sander across the top of the table he was currently building. The satin feel of the wood beneath his hands fed the artist inside him as nothing else could.

It had been six years since he'd picked up a paint-brush, faced a blank canvas and brought the images in his mind to life. And even now, that loss tore at him and his fingers wanted to curl around a slim wand of walnut and surround himself with the familiar scents of turpentine and linseed oil. He wouldn't—but the desire was always there, humming through his blood, through his dreams.

But though he couldn't paint, he also couldn't simply sit in the big house staring out windows, either.

So he'd turned his need for creativity, for creation, toward the woodworking that had always been a hobby. In this workshop, he built tables, chairs, small whimsical backyard lawn ornaments, and lost himself in the doing. He didn't have to think. Didn't have to remember.

Yet, today, his mind continuously drifted from the project at hand to the main house, where the woman was. It had been a long time since he'd had an attractive woman around for longer than an evening. And the prospect of Joy being in his house for the next month didn't make Sam happy. But damned if he could think of a way out of it. Sure, he could toss her and the girl out, but then what?

Memories of last December when he'd been on his own and damn near starved to death rushed into his brain. He didn't want to repeat that, but could he stand having a kid around all the time?

That thought brought him up short. He dropped the block sander onto the table, turned and looked out the nearest window to the house. The lights in the kitchen were on and he caught a quick glimpse of Joy moving through the room. Joy. Even her name went against everything he'd become. She was too much, he thought. Too beautiful. Too cheerful. Too tempting.

Well, hell. Recognizing the temptation she represented was only half the issue. Resisting her and what she made him want was the other half. She'd be right there, in his house, for a month. And he was still feeling that buzz of desire that had pumped into him from the moment he first saw her getting out of her car. He didn't want that buzz but couldn't ignore it, either.

When his cell phone rang, he dug it out of his pocket and looked at the screen. His mother. "Perfect. This day just keeps getting better."

Sam thought about not answering it, but he knew that Catherine Henry wouldn't be put off for long. She'd simply keep calling until he answered. Might as well get it over with.

"Hi, Mom."

"There's my favorite son," she said.

"Your *only* son," he pointed out.

"Hence the favorite," his mother countered. "You didn't want to answer, did you?"

He smiled to himself. The woman was practically psychic. Leaning one hip against the workbench, he said, "I did, though, didn't I?"

"Only because you knew I'd harangue you."

He rolled his eyes and started sanding again,

slowly, carefully moving along the grain. "What's up, Mom?"

"Kaye texted me to say she was off on her trip," his mother said. "And I wanted to see if Joy and Holly arrived all right."

He stopped, dropped the sander and stared out at the house where the woman and her daughter were busily taking over. "You knew?"

"Well, of course I knew," Catherine said with a laugh. "Kaye keeps me up to date on what's happening there since my favorite son tends to be a hermit and uncommunicative."

He took a deep breath and told himself that temper would be wasted on his mother. It would roll right on by, so there was no point in it. "You should have warned me."

"About what? Joy? Kaye tells me she's wonderful."

"About her daughter," he ground out, reminding himself to keep it calm and cool. He felt a sting of betrayal because his mother should have understood how having a child around would affect him.

There was a long pause before his mother said, "Honey, you can't avoid all children for the rest of your life."

He flinched at the direct hit. "I didn't say I was."

"Sweetie, you didn't have to. I know it's hard, but Holly isn't Eli."

He winced at the sound of the name he never allowed himself to so much as think. His hand tightened around the phone as if it were a lifeline. "I know that."

"Good." Her voice was brisk again, with that clipped tone that told him she was arranging everything in her mind. "Now that that's settled, you be nice. Kaye and I think you and Joy will get along very well."

He went completely still. "Is that right?"

"Joy's very independent and according to Kaye, she's friendly, outgoing—just what you need, sweetie. Someone to wake you up again."

Sam smelled a setup. Every instinct he possessed jumped up and shouted a warning even though it was too late to avoid what was already happening. Scraping one hand down his face, he shook his head and told himself he should have been expecting this. For years now, his mother had been nagging at him to move on. To accept the pain and to pick up the threads of his life.

She wanted him happy, and he understood that. What *she* didn't understand was that he'd already lost his shot at happiness. "I'm not interested, Mom."

"Sure you are, you just don't know it," his mother said in her crisp, no-nonsense tone. "And it's not like I've booked a church or expect you to sweep Joy off her feet, for heaven's sake. But would it kill you to be nice? Honestly, sweetie, you've become a hermit, and that's just not healthy."

Sam sighed heavily as his anger drained away. He

didn't like knowing that his family was worried about him. The last few years had been hard. On everyone. And he knew they'd all feel better about him if he could just pick up the threads of his life and get back to some sort of "normal." But a magical wave of his hands wasn't going to accomplish that.

The best he could do was try to convince his mother to leave him be. To let him deal with his own past in his own way. The chances of that, though, were slim. That was the burden of family. When you tried to keep them at bay for their own sake, they simply refused to go. Evidence: she and Kaye trying to play matchmaker.

But just because they thought they were setting him up with Joy didn't mean he had to go along. Which he wouldn't. Sure, he remembered that instant attraction he'd felt for Joy. That slam of heat, lust, that let him know he was alive even when he hated to acknowledge it. But it didn't change anything. He didn't want another woman in his life. Not even one with hair like sunlight and eyes the color of a summer sky.

And he for damn sure didn't want another child in his life.

What he had to do, then, was to make it through December, then let his world settle back into place. When nothing happened between him and Joy, his mother and Kaye would have to give up on the whole Cupid thing. A relief for all of them.

"Sam?" His mother's voice prompted a reaction

from him. "Have you slipped into a coma? Do I need to call someone?"

He laughed in spite of everything then told himself to focus. When dealing with Catherine Henry, a smart man paid attention. "No. I'm here."

"Well, good. I wondered." Another long pause before she said, "Just do me a favor, honey, and don't scare Joy off. If she's willing to put up with you for a month, she must really need the job."

Insulting, but true. Wryly, he said, "Thanks, Mom."

"You know what I mean." Laughing a little, she added, "That didn't come out right, but still. Hermits are *not* attractive, Sam. They grow their beards and stop taking showers and mutter under their breath all the time."

"Unbelievable," he muttered, then caught himself and sighed.

"It's already started," his mother said. "But seriously. People in those mountains are going to start telling their kids scary stories about the weird man who never leaves his house."

"I'm not weird," he argued. And he didn't have a beard. Just whiskers he hadn't felt like shaving in a few days. As far as muttering went, that usually happened only when his mother called.

"Not yet, but if things don't change, it's coming."

Scowling now, he turned away from the view of the house and stared unseeing at the wall opposite him. "Mom, you mean well. I know that."

"I do, sweetie, and you've got to—"

He cut her off, because really, it was the only way. "I'm already doing what I have to do, Mom. I've had enough change in my life already, thanks."

Then she was quiet for a few seconds as if she was remembering the pain of that major change. "I know. Sweetie, I know. I just don't want you to lose the rest of your life, okay?"

Sam wondered if it was all mothers or just his who refused to see the truth when it was right in front of them. He had nothing left to lose. How the hell could he have a life when he'd already lost everything that mattered? Was he supposed to forget? To pretend none of it had happened? How could he when every empty day reminded him of what was missing?

But saying any of that to his mother was a waste of time. She wouldn't get it. Couldn't possibly understand what it cost him every morning just to open his eyes and move through the day. They tried, he told himself. His whole family tried to be there for him, but the bottom line was, he was alone in this. Always would be.

And that thought told Sam he'd reached the end of his patience. "Okay, look, Mom, good talking to you, but I've got a project to finish."

"All right then. Just, think about what I said, okay?"

Hard not to when she said it every time she talked to him.

"Sure." A moment later he hung up and stuffed the phone back into his pocket. He shouldn't have answered it. Should have turned the damn thing off and forced her to leave a message. Then he wouldn't feel twisted up inside over things that could never be put right. It was better his way. Better to bury those memories, that pain, so deeply that they couldn't nibble away at him every waking moment.

A glance at the clock on the wall told him it was six and time for the dinner Joy had promised. Well, he was in no mood for company. He came and went when he liked and just because his temporary housekeeper made dinner didn't mean he had to show up. He scowled, then deliberately, he picked up the sander again and turned his focus to the wood. Sanding over the last coat of stain and varnish was meticulous work. He could laser in on the task at hand and hope it would be enough to ease the tension rippling through him.

It was late by the time he finally forced himself to stop working for the day. Darkness was absolute as he closed up the shop and headed for the house. He paused in the cold to glance up at the cloud-covered sky and wondered when the snow would start. Then he shifted his gaze to the house where a single light burned softly against the dark. He'd avoided the house until he was sure the woman and her daughter would be locked away in Kaye's rooms. For a second, he felt a sting of guilt for blowing off whatever dinner it was she'd made. Then again, he hadn't asked her to cook, had he? Hell, he hadn't even wanted her to stay. Yet somehow, she was.

Tomorrow, he told himself, he'd deal with her and lay out a few rules. If she was going to stay then she had to understand that it was the *house* she was supposed to take care of. Not him. Except for cooking—which he would eat whenever he damn well pleased—he didn't want to see her. For now, he wanted a shower and a sandwich. He was prepared for a can of soup and some grilled cheese.

Later, Sam told himself he should have known better. He opened the kitchen door and stopped in the doorway. Joy was sitting at the table with a glass of wine in front of her and turned her head to look at him when he walked in. "You're late."

That niggle of guilt popped up again and was just as quickly squashed. He closed and locked the door behind him. "I don't punch a clock."

"I don't expect you to. But when we say dinner's at six, it'd be nice if you showed up." She shrugged. "Maybe it's just me, but most people would call that 'polite.'"

The light over the stove was the only illumination and in the dimness, he saw her eyes, locked on him, the soft blond curls falling about her face. Most women he knew would have been furious with him for missing a dinner after he'd agreed to be there. But she wasn't angry, and that made him feel the twinge of guilt even deeper than he might have otherwise. But at the bottom of it, he didn't answer to her and it was just as well she learned that early on.

"Yeah," he said, "I got involved with a project and forgot the time." A polite lie that would go down better than admitting *I was avoiding you.* "Don't worry about it. I'll fix myself something."

"No you won't." She got up and walked to the oven. "I've kept it on warm. Why don't you wash up and have dinner?"

He wanted to say no. But damned if whatever she'd made didn't smell amazing. His stomach overruled his head and Sam surrendered. He washed his hands at the sink then sat down opposite her spot at the table.

"Did you want a glass of your wine?" she asked. "It's really good."

One eyebrow lifted. Wryly, he said, "Glad you approve."

"Oh, I like wine," she said, disregarding his tone. "Nothing better than ending your day with a glass and just relaxing before bed."

Bed. Not a word he should be thinking about when she was so close and looking so...edible. "Yeah. I'll get a beer."

"I'll get it," she said, as she set a plate of pasta in a thick red meat sauce in front of him.

The scent of it wafted to him and Sam nearly groaned. "What is that?"

"Baked mostaccioli with mozzarella and parmesan in my grandmother's meat sauce." She opened the fridge, grabbed a beer then walked back to the table. Handing it to him, she sat down, picked up her wineglass and had a sip.

"It smells great," he said grudgingly.

"Tastes even better," she assured him. Drawing one knee up, she propped her foot on her chair and looked at him. "Just so you know, I won't be waiting on you every night. I mean getting you a beer and stuff."

He snorted. "I'll make a note."

Then Sam took a bite and sighed. Whatever else Joy Curran was, the woman could *cook*. Whatever they had to talk about could wait, he thought, while he concentrated on the unexpected prize of a really great meal. So he said nothing else for a few bites, but finally sat back, took a drink of his beer and looked at her.

"Good?"

"Oh, yeah," he said. "Great."

She smiled and her face just—lit up. Sam's breath caught in his chest as he looked at her. That flash of something hot, something staggering, hit him again and he desperately tried to fight it off. Even while that strong buzz swept through him, remnants of the phone call with his mother rose up in his mind and he wondered if Joy had been in on whatever his mother and Kaye had cooking between them.

Made sense, didn't it? Young, pretty woman. Single mother. Why not try to find a rich husband?

Speculatively, he looked at her and saw sharp blue eyes without the slightest hint of guile. So maybe she wasn't in on it. He'd reserve judgment. For now. But whether she was or not, he had to set down some rules. If they were going to be living together for the next month, better that they both knew where they stood.

And, as he took another bite of her spectacular pasta, he admitted that he was going to let her stay— if only for the sake of his stomach.

"Okay," he said in between bites, "you can stay for the month."

She grinned at him and took another sip of her wine to celebrate. "That's great, thanks. Although, I wasn't really going to leave."

Amused, he picked up his beer. "Is that right?"

"It is." She nodded sharply. "You should know that I'm pretty stubborn when I want something, and I really wanted to stay here for the month."

He leaned back in his chair. The pale wash of the stove light reached across the room to spill across her, making that blond hair shine and her eyes gleam with amusement and determination. The house was quiet, and the darkness crouched just outside the window made the light and warmth inside seem almost intimate. Not a word he wanted to think about at the moment.

"Can you imagine trying to keep a five-year-old entertained in a tiny hotel room for a month?" She shivered and shook her head. "Besides being a living nightmare for me, it wouldn't be fair to Holly. Kids need room to run. Play."

He remembered. A succession of images flashed across his mind before he could stop them. As if the memories had been crouched in a corner, just waiting for the chance to escape, he saw pictures of another child. Running. Laughing. Brown eyes shining as he looked over his shoulder and—

Sam's grip on the beer bottle tightened until a part of him wondered why it didn't simply shatter in his hand. The images in his mind blurred, as if fingers of fog were reaching for them, dragging them back into the past where they belonged. Taking a slow, deep breath, he lifted the beer for a sip and swallowed the pain with it.

"Besides," she continued while he was still being dogged by memories, "this kitchen is amazing." Shaking her head, she looked around the massive room, and he knew what she was seeing. Pale oak cabinets, dark blue granite counters with flecks of what looked like abalone shells in them. Stainless steel appliances and sink and an island big enough to float to Ireland on. And the only things Sam ever really used on his own were the double-wide fridge and the microwave.

"Cooking in here was a treat. There's so much

space." Joy took another sip of wine. "Our house is so tiny, the kitchen just a smudge on the floor plan. Holly and I can't be in there together without knocking each other down. Plus there's the ancient plumbing and the cabinet doors that don't close all the way...but it's just a rental. One of these days, we'll get our own house. Nothing like this one of course, but a little bigger with a terrific kitchen and a table like this one where Holly can sit and do her homework while I make dinner—"

Briskly, he got back to business. It was either that or let her go far enough to sketch out her dream kitchen. "Okay, I get it. You need to be here, and for food like this, I'm willing to go along."

She laughed shortly.

He paid zero attention to the musical sound of that laugh or how it made her eyes sparkle in the low light. "So here's the deal. You can stay the month like we agreed."

"But?" she asked. "I hear a *but* in there."

"But." He nodded at her. "We steer clear of each other and you keep your daughter out of my way."

Her eyebrows arched. "Not a fan of kids, are you?"

"Not for a long time."

"Holly won't bother you," she said, lifting her wineglass for another sip.

"All right. Good. Then we'll get along fine." He finished off the pasta, savoring that last bite before taking one more pull on his beer. "You cook and clean. I spend most of my days out in the workshop, so we probably won't see much of each other anyway."

She studied him for several long seconds before a small smile curved her mouth and a tiny dimple appeared in her right cheek. "You're sort of mysterious, aren't you?"

Once again, she'd caught him off guard. And why did she look so pleased when he'd basically told her he didn't want her kid around and didn't particularly want to spend any time with *her*, either?

"No mystery. I just like my privacy is all."

"Privacy's one thing," she mused, tipping her head to one side to study him. "Hiding out's another."

"Who says I'm hiding?"

"Kaye."

He rolled his eyes. Kaye talked to his mother. To Joy. Who the hell *wasn't* she talking to? "Kaye doesn't know everything."

"She comes close, though," Joy said. "She worries about you. For the record, she says you're lonely, but private. Nice, but shut down."

He shifted in the chair, suddenly uncomfortable with the way she was watching him. As if she could look inside him and dig out all of his secrets.

"She wouldn't tell me why you've locked yourself away up here on the mountain—"

"That's something," he muttered, then remembered his mother's warning about hermits and muttering. Scowling, he took another drink of his beer.

"People do wonder, though," she mused. "Why you keep to yourself so much. Why you almost never go into town. I mean, it's beautiful here, but don't you miss talking to people?"

"Not a bit," he told her, hoping that statement would get her to back off.

"I really would."

"Big surprise," he muttered and then inwardly winced. Hell, he'd talked more in the last ten minutes than he had in the last year. Still, for some reason, he felt the need to defend himself and the way he lived. "I have Kaye to talk to if I desperately need conversation—which I don't. And I do get into town now and then." Practically never, though, he thought.

Hell, why should he go into Franklin and put up with being stared at and whispered over when he could order whatever he wanted online and have it shipped overnight? If nothing else, the twenty-first century was perfect for a man who wanted to be left the hell alone.

"Yeah, that doesn't happen often," she was saying. "There was actually a pool in town last summer—people were taking bets on if you'd come in at all before fall."

Stunned, he stared at her. "They were betting on me?"

"You're surprised?" Joy laughed and the sound

of it filled the kitchen. "It's a tiny mountain town with not a lot going on, except for the flood of tourists. Of course they're going to place bets on the local hermit."

"I'm starting to resent that word." Sam hadn't really considered that he might be the subject of so much speculation, and he didn't much care for it. What was he supposed to do now? Go into town more often? Or less?

"Oh," she said, waving one hand at him, "don't look so grumpy about it. If it makes you feel better, when you came into Franklin and picked up those new tools at the hardware store, at the end of August, Jim Bowers won nearly two hundred dollars."

"Good for him," Sam muttered, not sure how he felt about all of this. He'd moved to this small mountain town for the solitude. For the fact that no one would give a damn about him. And after five years here, he found out the town was paying close enough attention to him to actually lay money on his comings and goings. Shaking his head, he asked only, "Who's Jim Bowers?"

"He and his wife own the bakery."

"There's a bakery in Franklin?"

She sighed, shaking her head slowly. "It's so sad that you didn't know that."

A short laugh shot from his throat, surprising them both.

"You should do that more often," she said quietly.

"What?"

"Smile. Laugh. Lose the etched-in-stone-grumble expression."

"Do you have an opinion on everything?" he asked.

"Don't you?" she countered.

Yeah, he did. And his considered opinion on this particular situation was that he might have made a mistake in letting Joy and her daughter stay here for the next month.

But damned if he could regret it at the moment.

Three

By the following morning, Joy had decided the man needed to be pushed into getting outside himself. Sitting in the kitchen with him the night before had been interesting and more revealing than he would have liked, she was sure. Though he had a gruff, cold exterior, Joy had seen enough in his eyes to convince her that the real man was hidden somewhere beneath that hard shell he carried around with him.

She had known he'd been trying to avoid seeing her again by staying late in his workshop. Which was why she'd been waiting for him in the kitchen. Joy had always believed that it was better to face a problem head-on rather than dance around it and hope it would get better. So she'd been prepared to argue and bargain with him to make sure she and Holly could stay for the month.

And she'd known the moment he tasted her baked mostaccioli that arguments would not be necessary. He might not want her there, but her cooking had won him over. Clearly, he didn't like it, but he'd put up with her for a month if it meant he wouldn't starve. Joy could live with that.

What she might not be able to live with was her body's response to being near him. She hadn't expected that. Hadn't felt anything remotely like awareness since splitting with Holly's father before the little girl was born. And she wasn't looking for it now. She had a good life, a growing business and a daughter who made her heart sing. Who could ask for more than that?

But the man…intrigued her. She could admit, at least to herself, that sitting with him in the shadow-filled night had made her feel things she'd be better off forgetting. It wasn't her fault, of course. Just look at the man. Tall, dark and crabby. What woman wouldn't have a few fantasies about a man who looked like he did? Okay, normally she wouldn't enjoy the surly attitude—God knew she'd had enough "bad boys" in her life. But the shadows of old pain in his eyes told Joy that Sam hadn't always been so closed off.

So there was interest even when she knew there shouldn't be. His cold detachment was annoying, but the haunted look in his eyes drew her in. Made her want to comfort. Care. Dangerous feelings to have.

"Mommy, is it gonna snow today?"

Grateful for that sweet voice pulling her out of her circling thoughts, Joy walked to the kitchen table, bent down and kissed the top of her daughter's head.

"I don't think so, baby. Eat your pancakes now. And then we'll take a walk down to the lake."

"And skate?" Holly's eyes went bright with excitement at the idea. She forked up a bite of pancake and chewed quickly, eager now to get outside.

"We'll see if the lake's frozen enough, all right?" She'd brought their ice skates along since she'd known about the lake. And though she was no future competitor, Holly loved skating almost as much as she loved fairy princesses.

Humming, Holly nodded to herself and kept eating, pausing now and then for a sip of her milk. Her heels thumped against the chair rungs and sounded like a steady heartbeat in the quiet morning. Her little girl couldn't have been contained in a hotel room for a month. She had enough energy for three healthy kids and needed the room to run and play.

This house, this place, with its wide yard and homey warmth, was just what she needed. Simple as that. As for what Sam Henry made Joy feel? That would remain her own little secret.

"Hi, Sam!" Holly called out. "Mommy made pancakes. We're cellbrating."

"Celebrating," Joy corrected automatically, before she turned to look at the man standing in the open doorway. And darn it, she felt that buzz of awareness again the minute her gaze hit his. So tall, she thought with approval. He wore faded jeans and the scarred boots again, but today he wore a long-sleeved green thermal shirt with a gray flannel shirt over it. His too-long hair framed his face, and his eyes still carried the secrets that she'd seen in them the night before. They stared at each other as the seconds ticked past, and Joy wondered what he was thinking.

Probably trying to figure out the best way to get her and Holly to leave, she thought.

Well, that wasn't going to happen. She turned to the coffeemaker and poured him a cup. "Black?"

He accepted it. "How'd you guess?"

She smiled. "You look like the no-frills kind of man to me. Just can't imagine you ordering a half-caf, vanilla bean cappuccino."

He snorted, but took a long drink and sighed at the rush of caffeine in his system. Joy could appreciate that, since she usually got up a half hour before Holly just so she could have the time to enjoy that first, blissful cup of coffee.

"What're you celebrating?" he asked.

Joy flushed a little. "Staying here in the 'castle.'"

Holly's heels continued to thump as she hummed her way through breakfast. "We're having pancakes and then we're going skating on the lake and—"

"I said we'll see," Joy reminded her.

"Stay away from the lake."

Joy looked at him. His voice was low, brusque, and his tone brooked no argument. All trace of amusement was gone from eyes that looked as deep and dark as the night itself. "What?"

"The lake," he said, making an obvious effort to soften the hard note in his voice. "It's not solid enough. Too dangerous for either of you to be on it."

"Are you sure?" Joy asked, glancing out the kitchen window at the frigid world beyond the glass. Sure, it hadn't snowed much so far, but it had been below freezing every night for the last couple of weeks, so the lake should be frozen over completely by now.

"No point in taking the chance, is there? If it stays this cold, maybe you could try it in a week or two…"

Well, she thought, at least he'd accepted that she and Holly would still be there in two weeks. That was a step in the right direction, anyway. His gaze fixed on hers, deliberately avoiding looking at Holly, though the little girl was practically vibrating with barely concealed excitement. In his eyes, Joy saw real worry and a shadow of something darker, something older.

"Okay," she said, going with her instinct to ease whatever it was that was driving him. Reaching out, she laid one hand on his forearm and felt the tension gripping him before he slowly, deliberately pulled away. "Okay. No skating today."

"Moooommmmmyyyyy..."

How her daughter managed to put ten or more syllables into a single word was beyond her.

"We'll skate another day, okay, sweetie? How about today we take a walk in the forest and look for pinecones?" She kept her gaze locked on Sam's, so she actually saw relief flash across his eyes. What was it in his past that had him still tied into knots?

"Can we paint 'em for Christmas?"

"Sure we can, baby. We'll go after we clean the kitchen, so eat up." Then to Sam, she said, "How about some pancakes?"

"No, thanks." He turned to go.

"One cup of coffee and that's it?"

He looked back at her. "You're here to take care of the house. Not me."

"Not true. I'm also here to cook. For you." She smiled a little. "You should try the pancakes. They're really good, even if I do say so myself."

"Mommy makes the *best* pancakes," Holly tossed in.

"I'm sure she does," he said, still not looking at the girl.

Joy frowned and wondered why he disliked kids so much, but she didn't ask.

"Look, while you're here, don't worry about breakfast for me. I don't usually bother and if I change my mind I can take care of it myself."

"You're a very stubborn man, aren't you?"

He took another sip of coffee. "I've got a project to finish and I'm going out to get started on it."

"Well, you can at least take a muffin." Joy walked to the counter and picked a muffin—one of the batch she'd made just an hour ago—out of a ceramic blue bowl.

He sighed. "If I do, will you let me go?"

"If I do, will you come back?"

"I live here."

Joy smiled again and handed it over to him. "Then you are released. Go. Fly free."

His mouth twitched and he shook his head. "People think I'm weird."

"I don't." She said it quickly and wasn't sure why she had until she saw a quick gleam of pleasure in his eyes.

"Be sure to tell Kaye," he said, and left, still shaking his head.

"'Bye, Sam!" Holly's voice followed him and Joy was pretty sure he quickened his steps as if trying to outrun it.

Three hours later, Sam was still wishing he'd eaten those damn pancakes. He remembered the scent of them in the air, and his stomach rumbled in complaint. Pouring another cup of coffee from his workshop pot, he stared down at the small pile of blueberry muffin crumbs and wished he had another one. Damn it.

Wasn't it enough that Joy's face kept surfacing in his mind? Did she have to be such a good cook, too? And who asked her to make him breakfast? Kaye never did. Usually he made do with coffee and a power bar of some kind, and that was fine. Always had been anyway. But now he still had the lingering taste of that muffin in his mouth, and his stomach was still whining over missing out on pancakes.

But to eat them, he'd have had to take a seat at the table beside a chattering little girl. And all that sunshine and sweet innocence was just too much for Sam to take. He took a gulp of hot coffee and let the blistering liquid burn its way to the pit of his sadly empty stomach. And as hungry as he was, at least he'd completed his project. He leaned back against the workbench, crossed his feet at the ankles, stared at the finished table and gave himself a silent pat on the back.

In the overhead shop light, the wood gleamed and shone like a mirror in the sun. Every slender grain of the wood was displayed beautifully under the fresh coat of varnish, and the finish was smooth as glass. The thick pedestal was gnarled and twisted, yet it, too, had been methodically sanded until all the rough edges were gone as if they'd never been.

Taking a deadfall tree limb and turning it into the graceful pedestal of a table had taken some time, but it had been worth it. The piece was truly one of a kind, and he knew the people he'd made it for would approve. It was satisfying, seeing something in your head and creating it in the physical world. He used to do that with paint and canvas, bringing imaginary places to life, making them real.

Sam frowned at the memories, because remembering the passion he'd had for painting, the rush of starting something new and pushing himself to make it all perfect, was something he couldn't know now. Maybe he never would again. And that thought opened up a black pit at the bottom of his soul. But there was nothing he could do about it. Nothing that could ease that need, that bone-deep craving.

At least he had this, he told himself. Woodworking had given him, if not completion, then satisfaction. It filled his days and helped to ease the pain of missing the passion that had once driven his life. But then, he thought, once upon a time, his entire world had been different. The shame was, he hadn't really appreciated what he'd had while he had it. At least, he told himself, not enough to keep it.

He was still leaning against the workbench, studying the table, when a soft voice with a slight lisp asked, "Is it a fairy table?"

He swiveled his head to the child in the doorway. Her blond hair was in pigtails, she wore blue jeans, tiny pink-and-white sneakers with princesses stamped all over them and a pink parka that made her look impossibly small.

He went completely still even while his heart

raced, and his mind searched for a way out of there. Her appearance, on top of old memories that continued to dog him, hit him so hard he could barely take a breath. Sam looked into blue eyes the exact shade of her mother's and told himself that it was damned cowardly to be spooked by a kid. He had his reasons, but it was lowering to admit, even to himself, that his first instinct when faced with a child was to bolt.

Since she was still watching him, waiting for an answer, Sam took another sip of coffee in the hopes of steadying himself. "No. It's just a table."

"It looks like a tree." Moving warily, she edged a little farther into the workshop and let the door close behind her, shutting out the cold.

"It used to be," he said shortly.

"Did you make it?"

"Yes." She was looking up at him with those big blue eyes, and Sam was still trying to breathe. But his "issues" weren't her fault. He was being an ass, and even he could tell. He had no reason to be so short with the girl. How was she supposed to know that he didn't do kids anymore?

"Can I touch it?" she asked, giving him a winsome smile that made Sam wonder if females were *born* knowing how to do it.

"No," he said again and once more, he heard the sharp brusqueness in his tone and winced.

"Are you crabby?" She tilted her head to one side and looked up at him in all seriousness.

"What?"

Gloomy sunlight spilled through the windows that allowed views of the pines, the lake and the leaden sky that loomed threateningly over it all. The little girl, much like her mother, looked like a ray of sunlight in the gray, and he suddenly wished that she were anywhere but there. Her innocence, her easy smile and curiosity were too hard to take. Yet, her fearlessness at facing down an irritable man made her, to Sam's mind, braver than him.

"Mommy says when I'm crabby I need a nap." She nodded solemnly. "Maybe you need a nap, too."

Sam sighed. Also, like her mother, a bad mood wasn't going to chase her off. Accepting the inevitable, that he wouldn't be able to get rid of her by giving her one-word, bit-off answers, he said, "I don't need a nap, I'm just busy."

She walked into the workshop, less tentative now. Clearly oblivious to the fact that he didn't want her there, she wandered the shop, looking over the benches with tools, the stacks of reclaimed wood and the three tree trunks he had lined up along a wall. He should tell her to go back to the house. Wasn't it part of their bargain that the girl wouldn't bother him?

Hell.

"You don't look busy."

"Well, I am."

"Doing what?"

Sam sighed. Irritating, but that was a good question. Now that he'd finished the table, he needed to start something else. It wasn't only his hands he needed to keep busy. It was his mind. If he wasn't focusing on *something*, his thoughts would invariably track over to memories. Of another child who'd also had unending questions and bright, curious eyes. Sam cut that thought off and turned his attention to the tiny girl still exploring his workshop. Why hadn't he told her to leave? Why hadn't he taken her back to the house and told Joy to keep her away from him? Hell, why was he just standing there like a glowering statue?

"What's this do?"

The slight lisp brought a reluctant smile even as he moved toward her. She'd stopped in front of a vise that probably looked both interesting and scary to a kid.

"It's a wood vise," he said. "It holds a piece of wood steady so I can work on it."

She chewed her bottom lip and thought about it for a minute. "Like if I put my doll between my knees so I can brush her hair."

"Yeah," he said grudgingly. Smart kid. "It's sort of like that. Shouldn't you be with your mom?"

"She's cleaning and she said I could play in the yard if I stayed in the yard so I am but I wish it would snow and we could make angels and snowballs and a big snowman and—"

Amazed, Sam could only stare in awe as the little girl talked without seeming to breathe. Thoughts and words tumbled out of her in a rush that tangled together and yet somehow made sense.

Desperate now to stop the flood of high-pitched sounds, he asked, "Shouldn't you be in school?"

She laughed and shook her head so hard her pigtails flew back and forth across her eyes. "I go to pre-K cuz I'm too little for Big-K cuz my birthday comes too late cuz it's the day after Christmas and I can probably get a puppy if I ask Santa and Mommy's gonna get me a fairy doll for my birthday cuz Christmas is for the puppy and he'll be all white like a snowball and he'll play with me and lick me like Lizzie's puppy does when I get to play there and—"

So…instead of halting the rush of words and noise, he'd simply given her more to talk about. Sam took another long gulp of his coffee and hoped the caffeine would give him enough clarity to follow the kid's twisty thought patterns.

She picked up a scrap piece of wood and turned it over in her tiny hands.

"What can we make out of this?" she asked, holding it up to him, an interested gleam in her eye and an eager smile on her face.

Well, hell. He had nothing else to work on. It wasn't as though he was being drawn to the kid or anything. All he was doing was killing time. Keeping busy. Frowning to himself, Sam took the piece of wood from her and said, "If you're staying, take your jacket off and put it over there."

Her smile widened, her eyes sparkled and she hurried to do just what he told her. Shaking his head, Sam asked himself what he was doing. He should be dragging her back to the house. Telling her mother to keep the kid away from him. Instead, he was getting deeper.

"I wanna make a fairy house!"

He winced a little at the high pitch of that tiny voice and told himself that this didn't matter. He could back off again later.

Joy looked through the window of Sam's workshop and watched her daughter work alongside the man who had insisted he wanted nothing to do with her. Her heart filled when Holly turned a wide, delighted smile on the man. Then a twinge of guilt pinged inside her. Her little girl was happy and well-adjusted, but she was lacking a male role model in her life. God knew her father hadn't been interested in the job.

She'd told herself at the time that Holly would be better off without him than with a man who clearly didn't want to be a father. Yet here was another man who had claimed to want nothing to do with kids— her daughter in particular—and instead of complaining about her presence, he was working with her. Showing the little girl how to build...*something*. And Holly was loving it.

The little girl knelt on a stool at the workbench, following Sam's orders, and though she couldn't see what they were working on from her vantage point, Joy didn't think it mattered. Her daughter's happiness was evident, and whether he knew it or not, after only one day around Holly, Sam was opening up. She wondered what kind of man that opening would release.

The wind whipped past her, bringing the scent of snow, and Joy shivered deeper into her parka before walking into the warmth of the shop. With the blast of cold air announcing her presence, both Sam and Holly turned to look at her. One of them grinned. One of them scowled.

Of course.

"Mommy! Come and see, come and see!"

There was no invitation in Sam's eyes, but Joy ignored that and went to them anyway.

"It's a fairy house!" Holly squealed it, and Joy couldn't help but laugh. Everything these days was fairy. Fairy princesses. Fairy houses.

"We're gonna put it outside and the fairies can come and live in it and I can watch from the windows."

"That's a great idea."

"Sam says if I get too close to the fairies I'll scare 'em away," Holly continued, with an earnest look on her face. "But I wouldn't. I would be really quiet and they wouldn't see me or anything…"

"Sam says?" she repeated to the man standing there pretending he was somewhere else.

"Yeah," he muttered, rubbing the back of his neck. "If she watches through the window, she won't be out in the forest or—I don't know."

He was embarrassed. She could see it. And for some reason, knowing that touched her heart. The man who didn't want a child anywhere near him just spent two hours helping a little girl build a house for fairies. There was so much more to him than the face he showed to the world. And the more Joy discovered, the more she wanted to know.

Oh, boy.

"It's beautiful, baby." And it was. Small, but sturdy, it was made from mismatched pieces of wood and the roof was scalloped by layering what looked like Popsicle sticks.

"I glued it and everything, but Sam helped and he says I can put stuff in it for the fairies like cookies and stuff that they'll like and I can watch them…"

He shrugged. "She wanted to make something. I had some scrap wood. That's all."

"Thank you."

Impatience flashed across his face. "Not a big deal. And not going to be happening all the time, either," he added as a warning.

"Got it," Joy said, nodding. If he wanted to cling to that grumpy, don't-like-people attitude, she wouldn't fight him on it. Especially since she now knew it was all a front.

Joy took a moment to look around the big room. Plenty of windows would let in sunlight should the clouds ever drift away. A wide, concrete floor, scrupulously swept clean. Every kind of tool imaginable hung on the pegboards that covered most of two walls. There were stacks of lumber, most of it looking ragged and old—reclaimed wood—and there were deadfall tree trunks waiting for who knew what to be done to them.

Then she spotted the table and was amazed she hadn't noticed it immediately. Walking toward it, she sighed with pleasure as she examined it carefully, from the shining surface to the twisted tree limb base. "This is gorgeous," she whispered and whipped her head around to look at him. "You made this?"

He scowled again. Seemed to be his go-to expression. "Yeah."

"It's amazing, really."

"It's also still wet, so be careful. The varnish has to cure for a couple of days yet."

"I'm not touching."

"I didn't either, Mommy, did I, Sam?"

"Almost but not quite," he said.

Joy's fingers itched to stroke that smooth, sleek tabletop, so she curled her hands into fists to resist the urge. "I've seen some of your things in the gallery in town, and I loved them, too, by the way. But this." She shook her head and felt a real tug of possessiveness. "This I love."

"Thanks."

She thought the shadows in his eyes lightened a bit, but a second later, they were back so she couldn't be sure. "What are you working on next?"

"Like mother like daughter," he muttered.

"Curious?" she asked. "You bet. What are you going to do with those tree trunks?" The smallest of them was three feet around and two feet high.

"Work on them when I get a minute to myself." That leave-me-alone tone was back, and Joy decided not to push her luck any further. She'd gotten more than a few words out of him today and maybe they'd reached his limit.

"He's not mad, Mommy, he's just crabby."

Joy laughed.

Holly patted Sam's arm. "You could sing to him like you sing to me when I'm crabby and need a nap."

The look on Sam's face was priceless. Like he was torn between laughter and shouting and couldn't decide which way to go.

"What's that old saying?" Joy asked. "Out of the mouths of babes…"

Sam rolled his eyes and frowned. "That's it. Everybody out."

Still laughing, Joy said, "Come on, Holly, let's have some lunch. I made soup. Seemed like a good, cold day for it."

"You *made* soup?" he asked.

"Uh-huh. Beef and barley." She helped Holly get her jacket on, then zipped it closed against the cold wind. "Oh, and I made some beer bread, too."

"You made bread." He said it with a tinge of disbelief, and Joy couldn't blame him. Kaye didn't really believe in baking from scratch. Said it seemed like a waste when someone went to all the trouble to bake for her and package the bread in those nice plastic bags.

"Just beer bread. It's quick. Anyway," she said with a grin, "if you want lunch after your nap, I'll leave it on the stove for you."

"Funny."

Still smiling to herself, Joy took Holly's hand and led her out of the shop. She felt him watching her as they left and told herself that the heat swamping her was caused by her parka. And even she didn't believe it.

Four

Late at night, the big house was quiet, but not scary at all.

That thought made Joy smile to herself. She had assumed that a place this huge, with so many windows opening out onto darkness, would feel sort of like a horror movie. *Intrepid heroine wandering the halls of spooky house, alone, with nothing but a flashlight—until the battery dies.*

She shook her head and laughed at her own imagination. Instead of scary, the house felt like a safe haven against the night outside. Maybe it was the warmth of the honey-toned logs or maybe it was something else entirely. But one thing she was sure of was that she already loved it. Big, but not imposing, it was a happy house. Or would be if its owner wasn't frowning constantly.

But he'd smiled with Holly, Joy reminded herself as she headed down the long hallway toward the great room. He might have wished to be anywhere else, but he had been patient and kind to her little girl, and for Joy, nothing could have touched her more.

Her steps were quiet, her thoughts less so. She hadn't seen much of Sam since leaving him in the workshop. He'd deliberately kept his distance and Joy hadn't pushed. He'd had dinner, alone, in the dining room, then he'd disappeared again, barricading himself in the great room. She hadn't bothered him, had given him his space, and even now wouldn't be sneaking around his house if she didn't need something to read.

Holly was long since tucked in and Joy simply couldn't concentrate on the television, so she wanted to lose herself in a book. Keep her brain too busy to think about Sam. Wondering what his secrets were. Wondering what it would be like to kiss him. Wondering what the heck she was doing.

She threw a glance at the staircase and the upper floor, where the bedrooms were—where *Sam* was— and told herself to not think about it. Joy had spent the day cleaning the upstairs, though she had to admit that the man was so tidy, there wasn't much to straighten up.

But vacuuming and dusting gave her the chance

to see where he slept, how he lived. His bedroom was huge, offering a wide view of the lake and the army of pine trees that surrounded it. His bed was big enough for a family of four to sleep comfortably, and the room was decorated in soothing shades of slate blue and forest green. The attached bath had had her sighing in imagined pleasure.

A sea of pale green marble, from the floors to the counters, to the gigantic shower and the soaker whirlpool tub that sat in front of a bay window with a view of the treetops. He lived well, but so solitarily it broke her heart. There were no pieces of *him* in the room. No photos, no art on the wall, nothing to point to this being his *home*. As beautiful as it all was, it was still impersonal, as if even after living there for five years he hadn't left his own impression on the place.

He made her curious. Gorgeous recluse with a sexuality that made her want to drool whenever he was nearby. Of course, the logical explanation for her zip of reaction every time she saw the man was her self-imposed Man Fast. It had been so long since she'd been on a date, been kissed…heck, been *touched*, that her body was clearly having a breakdown. A shame that she seemed to be enjoying it so much.

Sighing a little, she turned, slipped into the great room, then came to a dead stop. Sam sat in one of the leather chairs in front of the stone fireplace, where flames danced across wood and tossed flickering shadows around the room.

Joy thought about leaving before he saw her. Yes, cowardly, but understandable, considering where her imaginings had been only a second or two ago. But even as she considered sneaking out, Sam turned his head and pinned her with a long, steady look.

"What do you need?"

Not exactly friendly, but not a snarl, either. Progress? She'd take it.

"A book." With little choice, Joy walked into the room and took a quick look around. This room was gorgeous during the day, but at night, with flickering shadows floating around…amazing. Really, was there anything prettier than firelight? When she shifted her gaze back to him, she realized the glow from the fire shining in his dark brown eyes was nearly hypnotic. Which was a silly thought to have, so she pushed it away fast. "Would you mind if I borrow a book? TV is just so boring and—"

He held up one hand to cut her off. "Help yourself."

"Ever gracious," she said with a quick grin. When he didn't return it, she said, "Okay, thanks."

She walked closer, surreptitiously sliding her gaze over him. His booted feet were crossed at the ankle, propped on the stone edge of the hearth. He was staring into the fire as if looking for something. The flickering light danced across his features, and she recognized the scowl that she was beginning to think was etched into his bones. "Everything okay?"

"Fine." He didn't look at her. Never took his gaze from the wavering flames.

"Okay. You've got a lot of books." She looked through a short stack of hardbacks on the table closest to him. A mix of mysteries, sci-fi and thrillers, mostly. Her favorites, too.

"Yeah. Pick one."

"I'm looking," she assured him, but didn't hurry as he clearly wanted her to. Funny, but the gruffer and shorter he became, the more intrigued she was.

Joy had seen him with Holly. She knew there were smiles inside him and a softness under the cold, hard facade. Yet he seemed determined to shut everyone out.

"Ew," she said as she quickly set one book aside. "Don't like horror. Too scary. I can't even watch scary movies. I get too involved."

"Yeah."

She smiled to herself at the one-word answer. He hadn't told her to get out, so she'd just keep talking and see what happened. "I tried, once. Went to the movies with a friend and got so scared and so tense I had to go sit in the lobby for a half hour."

She caught him give her a quick look. Interest. It was a start.

"I didn't go back into the theater until I convinced an usher to tell me who else died so I could relax."

He snorted.

Joy smiled, but didn't let him see it. "So I finally

went back in to sit with my friend, and even though I knew how it would end, I still kept my hands over my eyes through the rest of the movie."

"Uh-huh."

"But," she said, moving over to the next stack of books, "that doesn't mean I'm just a romantic comedy kind of girl. I like adventure movies, too. Where lots of things blow up."

"Is that right?"

Just a murmur, but he wasn't ignoring her.

"And the Avengers movies? Love those. But maybe it's just Robert Downey Jr. I like." She paused. "What about you? Do you like those movies?"

"Haven't seen them."

"Seriously?" She picked up a mystery she'd never read but instead of leaving with the book, she sat down in the chair beside his. "I think you're the first person I've ever met who hasn't seen those movies."

He spared her one long look. "I don't get out much."

"And isn't that a shame?"

"If I thought so," he told her, "I'd go out more."

Joy laughed at the logic. "Okay, you're right. Still. Heard of DVDs? Netflix?"

"You're just going to keep talking, aren't you?"

"Probably." She settled into her chair as if getting comfy for a long visit.

He shook his head and shifted his gaze back to

the fire as if that little discouragement would send her on her way.

"But back to movies," she said, leaning toward him over the arm of her chair. "This time of year I like all the Christmas ones. The gushier the better."

"Gushy."

It wasn't a question, but she answered anyway. "You know, the happy cry ones. Heck, I even tear up when the Grinch's heart grows at the end of that little cartoon." She sighed. "But to be fair, I've been known to get teary at a heart-tugging commercial at Christmastime."

"Yeah, I don't do Christmas."

"I noticed," she said, tipping her head to one side to study him. If anything, his features had tightened, his eyes had grown darker. Just the mention of the holiday had been enough to close him up tight. And still, she couldn't resist trying to reach him.

"When we're at home," she said, "Holly and I put up the Christmas decorations the day after Thanksgiving. You have to have a little restraint, don't you think? I mean this year, I actually saw Christmas wreaths for sale in *September*. That's going a little far for me and I love Christmas."

He swiveled a look at her. "If you don't mind, I don't really feel like talking."

"Oh, you don't have to. I like talking."

"No kidding."

She smiled and thought she saw a flicker of a response in his eyes, but if she had, it wasn't much of one because it faded away fast. "You can't get to know people unless you talk to them."

He scraped one hand across his face. "Yeah, maybe I don't want to get to know people."

"I think you do, you just don't want to want it."

"What?"

"I saw you today with Holly."

He shifted in his chair and frowned into the fire. "A one-time thing."

"So you said," Joy agreed, getting more comfortable in the chair, letting him know she wasn't going anywhere. "But I have to tell you how excited Holly was. She couldn't stop talking about the fairy house she built with you." A smile curved Joy's mouth. "She fell asleep in the middle of telling me about the fairy family that will move into it."

Surprisingly, the frown on his face deepened, as if hearing that he'd given a child happiness made him angry.

"It was a small thing, but it meant a lot to her. And to me. I wanted you to know that."

"Fine. You told me."

Outside, the wind kicked up, sliding beneath the eaves of the house with a sighing moan that sounded otherworldly. She glanced toward the front window at the night beyond, then turned back to the man with darkness in his eyes. She wondered what he was thinking, what he was seeing as he stared into the flames. Leaning toward him, she locked her hands around her up-drawn knees and said, "That wide front window is a perfect place for a Christmas tree, you know. The glass would reflect all the lights…"

His gaze shot to hers. "I already told you, I don't do Christmas."

"Sure, I get it," she said, though she really didn't. "But if you don't want to, Holly and I will take care of decorating and—"

He stood up, grabbed a fireplace poker and determinedly stabbed at the logs, causing sparks to fly and sizzle on their wild flight up the chimney. When he was finished, he turned a cold look on her and said, "No tree. No decorations. No Christmas."

"Wow. Speak of the Grinch."

He blew out a breath and glared at her, but it just didn't work. It was too late for him to try to convince her that he was an ogre or something. Joy had seen him with Holly. His patience. His kindness. Even though he hadn't wanted to be around the girl, he'd given her the gift of his time. Joy'd had a glimpse of the man behind the mask now and wouldn't be fooled again. Crabby? Yes. Mean? No.

"You're not here to celebrate the holidays," he reminded her in a voice just short of a growl. "You're here to take care of the house."

"I know. But, if you change your mind, I'm an excellent multitasker." She got to her feet and held on to the book she'd chosen from the stack. Staring up into his eyes, she said, "I'll do my job, but just so you know? You don't scare me, Sam, so you might as well quit trying so hard."

Every night, she came to the great room. Every night, Sam told himself not to be there. And every night, he was sitting by the fire, waiting for her.

Not like he was talking to her. But apparently *nothing* stopped *her* from talking. Not even his seeming disinterest in her presence. He'd heard about her business, about the house fire that had brought her to his place and about every moment of Holly's life up until this point. Her voice in the dark was both frustrating and seductive. Firelight created a cocoon of shadows and light, making it seem as if the two of them were alone in the world. Sam's days stretched out interminably, but the nights with Joy flew past, ending long before he wanted them to.

And that was an irritation, as well. Sam had been here for five years and in that time he hadn't wanted company. Hadn't wanted anyone around. Hell, he put up with Kaye because the woman kept his house running and meals on the table—but she also kept her distance. Usually. Now, here he was, sitting in the dark, waiting, *hoping* Joy would show up in the great room and shatter the solitude he'd fought so hard for.

But the days were different. During the day, Joy stayed out of his way and made sure her daughter did the same. They were like ghosts in the house.

Once in a while, he would catch a little girl's laughter, quickly silenced. Everything was clean, sheets on his bed changed, meals appeared in the dining room, but Joy herself was not to be seen. How she managed it, he wasn't sure.

Why it bothered him was even more of a mystery.

Hell, he hadn't wanted them to stay in the first place. Yet now that he wasn't being bothered, wasn't seeing either of them, he found himself always on guard. Expecting one or both of them to jump out from behind a door every time he walked through a room. Which was stupid, but kept him on edge. Something he didn't like.

Hell, he hadn't even managed to get started on his next project yet because thoughts of Joy and Holly kept him from concentrating on anything else. Today, he had the place to himself because Joy and Holly had gone into Franklin. He knew that because there'd been a sticky note on the table beside his blueberry muffin and travel mug of coffee that Joy routinely left out in the dining room every morning.

Strange. The first morning they were here, it was *him* avoiding having breakfast with them. Now, it seemed that Joy was perfectly happy shuffling him off without even seeing him. Why that bothered him, Sam didn't even ask himself. There was no damn answer anyway.

So now, instead of working, he found himself glancing out the window repeatedly, watching for

Joy's beat-up car to pull into the drive. All right, fine, it wasn't a broken-down heap, but her car was too old and, he thought, too unreliable for driving in the kind of snow they could get this high up the mountain. Frowning, he noted the fitful flurries of snowflakes drifting from the sky. Hardly a storm, more like the skies were teasing them with just enough snow to make things cold and slick.

So naturally, Sam's mind went to the road into town and the possible ice patches that dotted it. If Joy hit one of them, lost control of the car...his hands fisted. He should have driven them. But he hadn't really known they were going anywhere until it was too late. And that was because he wasn't spending any time with her except for those late-night sessions in the library.

Maybe if he'd opened his mouth the night before, she might have told him about this trip into town and he could have offered to drive them. Or at the very least, she could have driven his truck. Then he wouldn't be standing here wondering if her damn car had spun out.

Why the hell was he watching? Why did he care if she was safe or not? Why did he even bother to ask himself why? He knew damn well that his own past was feeding the sense of disquiet that clung to him. So despite resenting his own need to do it, he stayed where he was, watching. Waiting.

Which was why he was in place to see Ken Taylor

when he arrived. Taylor and his wife, Emma, ran the gallery/gift shop in Franklin that mostly catered to tourists who came up the mountain for snow skiing in winter and boating on the lake in summer. Their shop, Crafty, sold local artisans' work—everything from paintings to jewelry to candles to the hand-made furniture and decor that Sam made.

Grateful for the distraction, Sam shrugged into his black leather jacket and headed out of the workshop into the cold bite of the wind and swirl of snowflakes. Tugging the collar up around his neck, Sam squinted into the wind and walked over to meet the man as he climbed out of his truck.

"Hey, Sam." Ken held out one hand and Sam shook it.

"Thanks for coming out to get the table," Sam said. "Appreciate it."

"Hey, you keep building them, I'll drive up the mountain to pick them up." Ken grinned. About forty, he had pulled his black hair into a ponytail at the base of his neck. He wore a heavy brown coat over a flannel shirt, blue jeans and black work boots. He opened the gate at the back of his truck, then grinned at Sam. "One of these times, though, you should come into town yourself so you can see the reactions of the people who buy your stuff." Shaking his head, he mused, "I mean, they all but applaud when we bring in new stock."

"Good to know," Sam said. It was odd, he thought,

that he'd taken what had once been a hobby—wood-working—and turned it into an outlet for the creativity that had been choked off years ago. He liked knowing that his work was appreciated.

Once upon a time, he'd been lauded in magazines and newspapers. Reporters had badgered him for interviews, and one or two of his paintings actually hung in European palaces. He'd been the darling of the art world, and he'd enjoyed it all. He'd poured his heart and soul into his work and drank in the adulation as his due. Sam had so loved his work, he'd buried himself in it to the detriment of everything else. His life outside the art world had drifted past without him even realizing it.

Sam hadn't paid attention to what should have been most important, and before he could learn his lesson and make changes, he'd lost it and all he had left was the art. The paintings. The name he'd carved for himself. Left alone, it was only when he had been broken that he realized how empty it all was. How much he'd sacrificed for the glory.

So he wasn't interested in applause. Not anymore.

"No thanks," he said, forcing a smile in spite of his dark thoughts. He couldn't explain why he didn't want to meet prospective customers, why he didn't care about hearing praise, so he said, "I figure being the hermit on the mountain probably adds to the mystique. Why ruin that by showing up in town?"

Ken looked at him, as if he were trying to figure

him out, but a second later, shook his head. "Up to you, man. But anytime you change your mind, Emma would love to have you as the star of our next Meet the Artist night."

Sam laughed shortly. "Well, that sounds hideous."

Ken laughed, too. "I'll admit that it really is. Emma drives me nuts planning the snacks to get from Nibbles, putting out press releases, and the last time, she even bought some radio ads in Boise..." He trailed off and sighed. "And the artist managed to insult almost everyone in town. Don't understand these artsy types, but I'm happy enough to sell their stuff." He stopped, winced. "No offense."

"None taken," Sam assured him. "Believe me." He'd known plenty of the kind of artists Ken was describing. Those who so believed in their own press no one could stand to be around them.

"But, Emma loves doing it, of course, and I have to give it to her, we do big business on those nights."

Imagining being in the center of a crowd hungering to be close to an artist, to ask him questions, hang on everything he said, talk about the "art"... It all gave Sam cold chills and he realized just how far he'd come from the man he'd once been. "Yeah, like I said, awful."

"I even have to wear a suit. What's up with that?" Ken shook his head glumly and followed after Sam when he headed for the workshop door. "The only thing I like about it is the food, really. Nibbles has so many great things. My favorite's those tiny grilled cheese sandwiches. I can eat a dozen of 'em and still come back for more..."

Sam was hardly listening. He'd done so many of those "artist meets the public" nights years ago that he had zero interest in hearing about them now. His life, his *world*, had changed so much since then, he couldn't even imagine being a part of that scene anymore.

Ken was still talking. "Speaking of food, I saw Joy and Holly at the restaurant as I was leaving town."

Sam turned to look at him.

Ken shrugged. "Deb Casey and her husband, Sean, own Nibbles, and Deb and Joy are tight. She was probably in there visiting since they haven't seen each other in a while. How's it going with the two of them living here?"

"It's fine." What the hell else could he say? That Joy was driving him crazy? That he missed Holly coming into the workshop? That as much as he didn't want them there, he didn't want them gone even more? Made him sound like a lunatic. Hell, maybe he was.

Sam walked up to the table and drew off the heavy tarp he'd had protecting the finished table. Watery gray light washed through the windows and seemed to make the tabletop shine.

"Whoa." Ken's voice went soft and awe-filled. "Man, you've got some kind of talent. This piece is amazing. We're going to have customers outbidding each other trying to get it." He bent down, examined the twisted, gnarled branch pedestal, then stood again to admire the flash of the wood grain beneath the layers of varnish. "Dude, you could be in an art gallery with this kind of work."

Sam stiffened. He'd been in enough art galleries for a lifetime, he thought, and had no desire to do it again. That life had ultimately brought him nothing but pain, and it was best left buried in the past.

"Your shop works for me," he finally said.

Ken glanced at him. The steady look in his eyes told Sam that he was wondering about him. But that was nothing new. Everyone in the town of Franklin had no doubt been wondering about him since he first arrived and holed up in this house on the mountain. He had no answers to give any of them, because the man he used to be was a man even Sam didn't know anymore. And that's just the way he liked it.

"Well, maybe one day you'll explain to me what's behind you hiding out up here." Ken gave him a slap on the back. "Until then, though, I'd be a fool to complain when you're creating things like this for me to sell—and I'm no fool."

Sam liked Ken. The man was the closest thing to a friend Sam had had in years. And still, he couldn't bring himself to tell Ken about the past. About the mess he'd made of his life before finding this house on the mountain. So Sam concentrated instead on securing a tarp over the table and making sure it was tied down against the wind and dampness of the snow and rain. Ken helped him cover that with another tarp, wrapping this one all the way down and under the foot of the pedestal. Double protection since Sam really hated the idea of having the finish on the table ruined before it even made it into the shop. It took both of them to carry the table to the truck and secure it with bungee cords in the bed. Once it was done, Sam stuffed his hands into the pockets of his jacket and nodded to Ken as the man climbed behind the wheel.

"Y'know, I'm going to say this—just like I do every time I come out here—even knowing you'll say 'no, thanks.'"

Sam gave him a half smile, because he was ready for what was coming next. How could he not be? As Ken said, he made the suggestion every time he was here.

"Why don't you come into town some night?" the other man asked, forearm braced on the car door. "We'll get a couple beers, tell some lies..."

"No, thanks," Sam said and almost laughed at the knowing smile creasing Ken's face. If, for the first time, he was almost tempted to take the man up on it, he'd keep that to himself.

"Yeah, that's what I thought." Ken nodded and gave him a rueful smile. "But if you change your mind..."

"I'll let you know. Thanks for coming out to pick up the table."

"I'll let you know as soon as we sell it."

"I trust you," Sam said.

"Yeah, I wish that was true," Ken told him with another long, thoughtful look.

"It is."

"About the work, sure, I get that," Ken said. "But I want you to know, you can trust me beyond that, too. Whether you actually do or not."

Sam had known Ken and Emma for four years, and if he was looking for friendships, he couldn't do any better and he knew it. But getting close to people—be it Ken or Joy—meant allowing them close enough to know about his past. And the fewer people who knew, the less pity he had to deal with. So he'd be alone.

"Appreciate it." He slapped the side of the truck and took a step back.

"I'll see you, then."

Ken drove off and when the roar of his engine died away, Sam was left in the cold with only the sigh of the wind through the trees for company. Just the way he liked it.

Right?

Five

"Oh, God, look at her with that puppy," Joy said on a sigh.

Her heart filled and ached as she watched Holly laughing at the black Lab puppy jumping at her legs. How could one little girl mean so much? Joy wondered.

When she'd first found herself pregnant, Joy remembered the rush of pleasure, excitement that she'd felt. It hadn't mattered to her that she was single and not exactly financially stable. All she'd been able to think was, she would finally have her own family. Her child.

Joy had been living in Boise back then, starting up her virtual assistant business and working with several of the small businesses in town. One of those was Mike's Bikes, a custom motorcycle shop owned by Mike Davis.

Mike was charming, handsome and had the whole bad-boy thing going for him, and Joy fell hard and fast. Swept off her feet, she gave herself up to her first real love affair and thought it would be forever. It lasted until the day she told Mike she was pregnant, expecting to see the same happiness in him that she was feeling. Mike, though, had no interest in being anyone's father—or husband, if it came to that. He told her they were through. She was a good time for a while, but the good time was over. He signed a paper relinquishing all future rights to the child he'd created and Joy walked away.

When she was a kid, she'd come to Franklin with a foster family for a long weekend in the woods and she'd never forgotten it. So when she needed a fresh start for her and her baby, Joy had come here, to this tiny mountain town. And here is where she'd made friends, built her family and, at long last, had finally felt as though she belonged.

And of all the things she'd been gifted with since moving here, Deb Casey, her best friend, was at the top of the list.

Deb Casey walked to Joy and looked out the window at the two little girls rolling around on the winter brown grass with a fat black puppy. Their laughter and the puppy's yips of excitement brought a quick smile. "She's as crazy about that puppy as my Lizzie."

"I know." Joy sighed a little and leaned on her friend's kitchen counter. "Holly's telling everyone she's getting a puppy of her own for Christmas."

"A white one," Deb supplied.

Rolling her eyes, Joy shook her head. "I've even been into Boise looking for a white puppy, and no one has any. I guess I'm going to have to start preparing her for the fact that Santa can't always bring you what you want."

"Oh, I hate that." Deb turned back to the wide kitchen island and the tray of tiny brownies she was finishing off with swirls of white chocolate icing. "You've still got a few weeks till Christmas. You might find one."

"I'll keep looking, sure. But," Joy said, resigned, "she might have to wait."

"Because kids wait so well," Deb said with a snort of laughter.

"You're not helping."

"Have a brownie. That's the kind of help you need."

"Sold." Joy leaned in and grabbed one of the tiny brownies that was no more than two bites of chocolate heaven.

The brownies, along with miniature lemon meringue pies, tiny chocolate chip cookies and miniscule Napoleons, would be filling the glass cases at

Nibbles by this afternoon. The restaurant had been open for only a couple of years, but it had been a hit from the first day. Who wouldn't love going for lunch where you could try four or five different types of sandwiches—none of them bigger than a bite or two? Gourmet flavors, a fun atmosphere and desserts that could bring a grown woman to tears of joy, Nibbles had it all.

"Oh, God, this should be illegal," Joy said around a mouthful of amazing brownie.

"Ah, then I couldn't sell them." Deb swirled white chocolate on a few more of the brownies. "So, how's it going up there with the Old Man of the Mountain?"

"He's not old."

"No kidding." Deb grinned. "I saw him sneaking into the gallery last summer, and I couldn't believe it. It was like catching a glimpse of a unicorn. A gorgeous unicorn, I've got to say."

Joy took another brownie and bit into it. *Gorgeous* covered it. Of course, there was also *intriguing*, *desirable*, *fascinating*, and as yummy as this brownie. "Yeah, he is."

"Still." Deb looked up at Joy. "Could he be more antisocial? I mean, I get why and all, but aren't you going nuts up there with no one to talk to?"

"I talk to him," Joy argued.

"Yes, but does he talk back?"

"Not really, though in his defense, I do talk a lot." Joy shrugged. "Maybe it's hard for him to get a word in."

"Not that hard for me."

"We're women. Nothing's that hard for us."

"Okay, granted." Deb smiled, put the frosting back down and planted both hands on the counter. "But what's really going on with you? I notice you're awful quick to defend him. Your protective streak is coming out."

That was the only problem with a best friend, Joy thought. Sometimes they saw too much. Deb knew that Joy hadn't dated anyone in years. That she hadn't had any interest in sparking a relationship—since her last one had ended so memorably. So of course she would pick up on the fact that Joy was suddenly very interested in one particular man.

"It's nothing."

"Sure," Deb said with a snort of derision. "I believe that."

"Fine, it's *something*," Joy admitted. "I'm not sure what, though."

"But he's so not the kind of guy I would expect you to be interested in. He's so—cold."

Oh, there was plenty of heat inside Sam Henry. He just kept it all tamped down. Maybe that's what drew her to him, Joy thought. The mystery of him. Most men were fairly transparent, but Sam had hidden depths that practically demanded she unearth them. She couldn't get the image of the shadows in his eyes out of her mind. She wanted to know why he was so shut down. Wanted to know how to open him up.

Smiling now, she said, "Holly keeps telling me he's not mean, he's just crabby."

Deb laughed. "Is he?"

"Oh, definitely. But I don't know why."

"I might."

"What?"

Deb sighed heavily. "Okay, I admit that when you went to stay up there, I was a little worried that maybe he was some crazed weirdo with a closet full of women's bones or something."

"I keep telling you, stop watching those horror movies."

Deb grinned. "Can't. Love 'em." She picked up the frosting bag as if she needed to be doing something while she told the story. "Anyway, I spent a lot of time online, researching the local hermit and—"

"What?" And why hadn't Joy done the same thing? Well, she knew why. It had felt like a major intrusion on his privacy. She'd wanted to get him to actually *tell* her about himself. Yet here she was now, ready to pump Deb for the information she herself hadn't wanted to look for.

"You know he used to be a painter."

"Yes, that much I knew." Joy took a seat at one of the counter stools and kept her gaze fixed on Deb's blue eyes.

"He was famous. I mean *famous*." She paused for

emphasis. "Then about five years ago, he just stopped painting entirely. Walked away from his career and the fame and fortune and moved to the mountains to hide out."

"You're not telling me anything I didn't know so far."

"I'm getting there." Sighing, Deb said softly, "His wife and three-year-old son died in a car wreck five years ago."

Joy felt as though she'd been punched in the stomach. The air left her lungs as sympathetic pain tore at her. Tears welled in her eyes as she tried to imagine that kind of hell. That kind of devastation. "Oh, my God."

"Yeah, I know," Deb said with a wince. Laying down the pastry bag, she added, "When I found out, I felt so bad for him."

Joy did, too. She couldn't even conceive the level of pain Sam had experienced. Even the thought of such a loss was shattering. Remembering the darkness in his eyes, Joy's heart hurt for him and ached to somehow ease the grief that even five years later still held him in a tight fist. Now at least she could understand a little better why he'd closed himself off from the world.

He'd hidden himself away on a mountaintop to escape the pain that was stalking him. She saw it in his eyes every time she looked at him. Those shadows that were a part of him were really just reflections of the pain that was in his heart. Of *course* he was still feeling the soul-crushing pain of losing his family. God, just the thought of losing Holly was enough to bring her to her knees.

Instinctively, she moved to Deb's kitchen window and looked out at two little girls playing with a puppy. Her gaze locked on her daughter, Joy had to blink a sheen of tears from her eyes. So small. So innocent. To have that...*magic* winked out like a blown-out match? She couldn't imagine it. Didn't want to try.

"God, this explains so much," she whispered.

Deb walked to her side. "It does. But Joy, before you start riding to the rescue, think about it. It's been five years since he lost his family, and as far as I know, he's never talked about it. I don't think anyone in town even knows about his past."

"Probably not," she said, "unless they took the time to do an internet search on him."

Deb winced again. "Maybe I shouldn't have. Sort of feels like intruding on his privacy, now that I know."

"No, I'm glad you did. Glad you told me," Joy said, with a firm shake of her head. "I just wish I'd thought of doing it myself. Heck, I'm on the internet all the time, just working."

"That's why it didn't occur to you," Deb told her. "The internet is work for you. For the rest of us, it's a vast pool of unsubstantiated information."

She had a point. "Well, then I'm glad I came by today to get your updates for your website."

As a virtual assistant, Joy designed and managed websites for most of the shops in town, plus the medical clinic, plus she worked for a few mystery authors who lived all over the country. It was the perfect job for her, since she was very good at computer programming and it allowed her to work at home and be with Holly instead of sending the little girl out to day care.

But, because she spent so much time online for her job, she rarely took the time to browse sites for fun. Which was why it hadn't even occurred to her to look up Sam Henry.

Heart heavy, Joy looked through the window and watched as Holly fell back onto the dry grass, laughing as the puppy lunged up to lavish kisses on her face. Holly. God, Joy thought, now she knew why Sam had demanded she keep her daughter away from him. Seeing another child so close to the age of his lost son must be like a knife to the heart.

And yet…she remembered how kind he'd been with Holly in the workshop that first day. How he'd helped her, how Holly had helped *him*.

Sam hadn't thrown Holly out. He'd spent time with her. Made her feel important and gave her the satisfaction of building something. He had closed himself off, true, but there was clearly a part of him looking for a way out.

She just had to help him find it.

Except for her nightly monologues in the great room, Joy had been giving him the space he claimed to want. But now she thought maybe it wasn't space he needed...but less of it. He'd been alone too long, she thought. He'd wrapped himself up in his pain and had been that way so long now, it probably felt normal to him. So, Joy told herself, if he wouldn't go into the world, then the world would just have to go to him.

"You're a born nurturer," Deb whispered, shaking her head.

Joy looked at her.

"I can see it on your face. You're going to try to 'save' him."

"I didn't say that."

"Oh, honey," Deb said, "you didn't have to."

"It's annoying to be read so easily."

"Only because I love you." Deb smiled. "But Joy, before you jump feetfirst into this, maybe you should consider that Sam might not *want* to be saved."

She was sure Deb was right. He didn't want to come out of the darkness. It had become his world. His, in a weird way, comfort zone. That didn't make it right.

"Even if he doesn't want it," Joy murmured, "he needs it."

"What *exactly* are you thinking?" Deb asked.

Too many things, Joy realized. Protecting Holly, reaching Sam, preparing for Christmas, keeping up with all of the holiday work she had to do for her clients... Oh, whom was she kidding? At the moment, Sam was uppermost in her mind. She was going to drag him back into the land of the living, and she had the distinct feeling he was going to put up a fight.

"I'm thinking that maybe I'm in way over my head."

Deb sighed a little. "How deep is the pool?"

"Pretty deep," Joy mused, thinking about her reaction to him, the late-night talks in the great room where it was just the two of them and the haunted look in his eyes that pulled at her.

Deb bumped her hip against Joy's. "I see that look in your eyes. You're already attached."

She was. Pointless to deny it, especially to Deb of all people, since she could read Joy so easily.

"Yes," she said and heard the worry in her own voice, "but like I said, it's pretty deep waters."

"I'm not worried," Deb told her with a grin. "You're a good swimmer."

That night, things were different.

When Sam came to dinner in the dining room, Joy and Holly were already seated, waiting for him. Since every other night, the two of them were in the kitchen, he looked thrown for a second. She gave him a smile even as Holly called out, "Hi, Sam!"

If anything, he looked warier than just a moment before. "What's this?"

"It's called a communal meal," Joy told him, serving up a bowl of stew with dumplings. She set the bowl down at his usual seat, poured them both a glass of wine, then checked to make sure Holly was settled beside her.

"Mommy made dumplings. They're really good," the little girl said.

"I'm sure." Reluctantly, he took a seat then looked at Joy. "This is not part of our agreement."

He looked, she thought, as if he were cornered. Well, good, because he was. Dragging him out of the darkness was going to be a step-by-step journey— and it started now.

"Actually…" she told him, spooning up a bite of her own stew, then sighing dramatically at the taste. Okay, yes she was a good cook, but she was putting it on for his benefit. And it was working. She saw him glance at the steaming bowl in front of his chair, even though he hadn't taken a bite yet. "…our agreement was that I clean and cook. We never agreed to not eat together."

"It was implied," he said tightly.

"Huh." She tipped her head to one side and studied the ceiling briefly as if looking for an answer there. "I didn't get that implication at all. But why don't you eat your dinner and we can talk about it."

"It's good, Sam," Holly said again, reaching for her glass of milk.

He took a breath and exhaled on a sigh. "Fine. But this doesn't mean anything."

"Of course not," Joy said, hiding the smile blossoming inside her. "You're still the crabby man we all know. No worries about your reputation."

His lips twitched as he tasted the stew. She waited for his reaction and didn't have to wait long. "It's good."

"Told ya!" Holly's voice was a crow of pleasure.

"Yeah," he said, flicking the girl an amused glance. "You did."

Joy saw that quick look and smiled inside at the warmth of it.

"When we went to town today I played with Lizzie's puppy," Holly said, taking another bite and wolfing it down so she could keep talking. "He licked me in the face again and I laughed and Lizzie and me ran and he chased us and he made Lizzie fall but she didn't cry…"

Joy smiled at her daughter, loving how the girl could launch into a conversation that didn't need a partner, commas or periods. She was so thrilled by life, so eager to experience everything, just watching her made Joy's life better in every possible way. From the corner of her eye, she stole a look at Sam and saw the flicker of pain in his eyes. It had to be hard for him to listen to a child's laughter and have to grieve for the loss of his own child. But he couldn't avoid children forever. He'd end up a miserable old man, and that would be a waste, she told herself.

"And when I get my puppy, Lizzie can come and play with it, too, and it will chase us and mine will be white cuz Lizzie's is black and it would be fun to have puppies like that…"

"She's really counting on that puppy," Joy murmured.

"So?" Sam dipped into his stew steadily as if he was hurrying to finish so he could escape the dining room—and their company.

Deliberately, Joy refilled his bowl over his complaints.

"So, there aren't any white puppies to be had," she whispered, her own voice covered by the rattle of Holly's excited chatter.

"Santa's going to bring him, remember, Mommy?" Holly asked, proving that her hearing was not affected by the rush of words tumbling from her own mouth.

"That's right, baby," Joy said with a wince at Sam's smirk. "But you know, sometimes Santa can't bring everything you want—"

"If you're not a good girl," Holly said, nodding sharply. "But I am a good girl, right, Mommy?"

"Right, baby." She was really stuck now. Joy was going to have to go into Boise and look for a puppy or she was going to have a heartbroken daughter on Christmas morning, and that she couldn't allow.

Too many of Joy's childhood Christmases had been empty, lonely. She never wanted Holly to feel the kind of disappointment Joy had known all too often.

"I told Lizzie about the fairy house we made, Sam, and she said she has fairies at her house, but I don't think so cuz you need lots of trees for fairies and there's not any at Lizzie's..."

"The kid never shuts up," Sam said, awe in his voice.

"She's excited." Joy shrugged. "Christmas is coming."

His features froze over and Joy could have kicked herself. Sure, she planned on waking him up to life, but she couldn't just toss him into the middle of a fire, could she? She had to ease him closer to the warmth a little at a time.

"Yeah."

"I know you said no decorations or—"

His gaze snapped to hers, cold. Hard. "That's right."

"In the great room," she continued as if he hadn't said a word, as if she hadn't gotten a quick chill from the ice in his eyes, "but Holly and I are here for the whole month and a little girl needs Christmas. So we'll keep the decorations to a minimum."

His mouth worked as if he wanted to argue and couldn't find a way to do it without being a complete jerk. "Fine."

She reached out and gave his forearm a quick pat.

Even with removing her hand almost instantly, that swift buzz of something amazing tingled her fingers. Joy took a breath, smiled and said, "Don't worry, we won't be too happy around you, either. Wouldn't want you upset by the holiday spirit."

He shot her a wry look. "Thanks."

"No problem." Joy grinned at him. "You have to be careful or you could catch some stray laugh and maybe even try to join in only to have your face break."

Holly laughed. "Mommy, that's silly. Faces can't break, can they, Sam?"

His brown eyes were lit with suppressed laughter, and Joy considered that a win for her. "You're right, Holly. Faces can't break."

"Just freeze?" Joy asked, her lips curving.

"Yeah. I'm good at freezing," he said, gaze meeting hers in a steady stare.

"That's cuz it's cold," Holly said, then added, "Can I be done now, Mommy?"

Joy tore her gaze from his long enough to check that her daughter had eaten most of her dinner. "Yes, sweetie. Why don't you go get the pinecones we found today and put them on the kitchen counter? We'll paint them after I clean up."

"Okay!" The little girl scooted off the chair, ran around the table and stopped beside Sam. "You wanna paint with me? We got glitter, too, to put on the pinecones and we get to use glue to stick it."

Joy watched him, saw his eyes soften, then saw him take a deliberate, emotional step back. Her heart hurt, remembering what she now knew about his past. And with the sound of her daughter's high-pitched, excited voice ringing in the room, Joy wondered again how he'd survived such a tremendous loss. But even as she thought it, Joy realized that he was like a survivor of a disaster.

He'd lived through it but he wasn't *living*. He was still existing in that half world of shock and pain, and it looked to her as though he'd been there so long he didn't have a clue how to get out. And that's where Joy came in. She wouldn't leave him in the dark. Couldn't watch him let his life slide past.

"No, thanks." Sam gave the little girl a tight smile. "You go ahead. I've got some things I've got to do."

Well, at least he didn't say anything about hating Christmas. "Go ahead, sweetie. I'll be there in a few minutes."

"Okay, Mommy. 'Bye, Sam!" Holly waved, turned and raced toward the kitchen, eager to get started on those pinecones.

When they were alone again, Joy looked at the man opposite her and smiled. "Thanks for not popping her Christmas balloon."

He scowled at her and pushed his empty bowl to one side. "I'm not a monster."

"No," she said, thoughtfully. "You're not."

He ignored that. "Look, I agreed to you and Holly

doing Christmas stuff in your part of the house. Just don't try to drag me into it. Deal?"

She held out one hand and left it there until he took it in his and gave it a firm shake. Of course, she had no intention of keeping to that "deal." Instead, she was going to wake him up whether he liked it or not. By the time she was finished, Joy assured herself, he'd be roasting chestnuts in the fireplace and stringing lights on a Christmas tree.

His eyes met hers and in those dark depths she saw…everything. A tingling buzz shot up her arm and ricocheted around in the center of her chest like a Ping-Pong ball in a box. Her heartbeat quickened and her mouth went dry. Those eyes of his gazed into hers, and Joy took a breath and held it. Finally, he let go of her hand and took a single step back as if to keep a measure of safe distance between them.

"Well," she said when she was sure her voice would work again, "I'm going to straighten out the kitchen then paint pinecones with my daughter."

"Right." He scrubbed one hand across his face. "I'll be in the great room."

She stood up, gathered the bowls together and said, "Earlier today, Holly and I made some Christmas cookies. I'll bring you a few with your coffee."

"Not necessary—"

She held up one hand. "You can call them winter cookies if it makes you feel better."

He choked off a laugh, shook his head and started

out of the room. Before he left, he turned to look back at her. "You don't stop, do you?"

"Nope." He took another step and paused when she asked, "The real question is, do you want me to?"

He didn't speak, just gave her a long look out of thoughtful, chocolate-brown eyes, then left the room. Joy smiled to herself, because that nonanswer told her everything she wanted to know.

Six

Sam used to hate the night.

The quiet. The feeling of being alone in the world. The seemingly endless hours of darkness. It had given him too much time to think. To remember. To torture himself with what-might-have-beens. He couldn't sleep because memories became dreams that jolted him awake—or worse, lulled him into believing the last several years had never really happened. Then waking up became the misery, and so the cycle went.

Until nearly a week ago. Until Joy.

He had a fire blazing in the hearth as he waited for her. Night was now something he looked forward to. Being with her, hearing her voice, her laughter, had become the best part of his days. He enjoyed her quick mind, and her sense of humor—even when it was directed at him. He liked hearing her talk about what was happening in town, even though he didn't know any of the people she told him about. He liked seeing her with her daughter, watching the love between them, even though it was like a knife to his heart.

Sam hadn't expected this, hadn't thought he wanted it. He rubbed his palms together, remembering the flash of heat that enveloped him when he'd taken her hand to seal their latest deal. He could see the flash in her eyes that told him she'd felt the same damn thing. And with the desire gripping him, guilt speared through Sam, as well. Everything he'd lost swam in his mind, reminding him that *feeling*, *wanting*, was a steep and slippery road to loss.

He stared into the fire, listened to the hiss and snap of flame on wood, and for the first time in years, he *tried* to bring those long-abandoned memories to the surface. Watching the play of light and shadow, the dance of flames, Sam fought to draw his dead wife's face into his mind. But the memory was indistinct, as if a fog had settled between them, making it almost impossible for him to remember just the exact shade of her brown eyes. The way her mouth curved in a smile. The fall of her hair and the set of her jaw when she was angry.

It was all…hazy, and as he battled to remember Dani, it was Joy's face that swam to the surface of his mind. The sound of *her* laughter. The scent of her. And he wanted to know the taste of her. What the hell was happening to him and why was he allowing it? Sam told himself to leave. To not be there when Joy came into the room. But as much as he knew he should, he also knew he wouldn't.

"I brought more cookies."

He turned in his chair to look at her, and even from across the room, he felt that now-familiar punch of awareness. Of heat. And he knew it was too late to leave.

At her smile, one eyebrow lifted and he asked, "More reindeer and Santas?"

That smile widened until it sparkled in her eyes. She walked toward him, carrying a tray that held the plate of cookies and two glasses of golden wine.

"This time we have snowmen and wreaths and—" she paused "—*winter* trees."

He shook his head and sighed. It seemed she was determined to shove Christmas down his throat whether he liked it or not. "You're relentless."

Why did he like that about her?

"That's been said before," she told him and took her usual seat in the chair beside his. Setting the tray down on the table between them, she took a cookie then lifted her glass for a sip of wine.

"Really. Cookies and wine."

"Separately, they're both good," she said, waving

her cookie at the plate, challenging him to join her. "Together, they're amazing."

The cookies were good, Sam thought, reaching out to pick one up and bite in. All he'd had to do was close his eyes so he wasn't faced with iced, sprinkled Santas and they were just cookies. "Good."

"Thanks." She sat back in the chair. "That wasn't so hard, was it?"

"What?"

"Talking to me." She folded her legs up beneath her, took another sip of her wine and continued. "We've been sitting in this room together for five nights now and usually, the only voice I hear is my own."

He frowned, took the wine and drank. Gave him an excuse for not addressing that remark. Of course, it was true, but that wasn't the point. He hadn't asked her to join him every night, had he? When she only looked at him, waiting, he finally said, "Didn't seem to bother you any."

"Oh, I don't mind talking to myself—"

"No kidding."

She grinned. "But it's more fun talking to other people."

Sam told himself not to notice how her hair shined golden in the firelight. How her eyes gleamed and her mouth curved as if she were always caught on the verge of a smile. His gaze dropped to the plain blue shirt she wore and how the buttons pulled across her chest. Her jeans were faded and soft, clinging to her legs as she curled up and got comfortable. Red polish decorated her toes. Why that gave him a quick, hot jolt, he couldn't have said.

Everything in him wanted to pull her out of that chair, wrap his arms around her and take her tantalizing mouth in a kiss that would sear both of them. And *why*, he asked himself, did he suddenly feel like a cheating husband? Because since Dani, no other woman had pulled at him like this. And even as he wanted Joy, he hated that he wanted her. The cookie turned to chalk in his mouth and he took a sip of wine to wash it down.

"Okay, someone just had a dark thought," she mused.

"Stay out of my head," Sam said, slanting her a look.

Feeling desire didn't mean that he welcomed it. Life had been—not easier—but more clear before Joy walked into his house. He'd known who he was then. A widower. A father without a child. And he'd wrapped himself up in memories designed to keep him separate from a world he wasn't interested in anyway.

Yet now, after less than a week, he could feel those layers of insulation peeling away and he wasn't sure how to stop it or even if he wanted to. The shredding of his cloak of invisibility was painful and still he couldn't stop it.

Dinner with Joy and Holly had tripped him up, too, and he had a feeling she'd known it would. If he'd been smart, he would have walked out of the room as soon as he'd seen them at the table. But one look into Joy's and Holly's eyes had ended that idea before it could begin. So instead of having his solitary meal, he'd been part of a unit—and for a few minutes, he'd enjoyed it. Listening to Holly's excited chatter, sharing knowing looks with Joy. Then, of course, he remembered that Joy and Holly weren't *his*. And that was what he had to keep in mind.

Taking another drink of the icy wine, he shifted his gaze to the fire. Safer to look into the flames than to stare at the deep blue of her eyes. "Yeah," he said, finally responding to her last statement, "I don't really talk to people anymore."

"No kidding." She threw his earlier words back at him, and Sam nodded at the jab.

"Kaye tends to steer clear of me most of the time."

"Kaye doesn't like talking to people, either," Joy said, laughing. "You two are a match made in heaven."

"There's a thought," he muttered.

She laughed again, and the sound of it filled every empty corner of the room. It was both balm and torture to hear it, to know he *wanted* to hear it. How was it possible that she'd made such an impact on him in such a short time? He hadn't even noticed her worming her way past his defenses until it was impossible to block her.

"So," she asked suddenly, pulling him from his thoughts, "any idea where I can find a puppy?"

"No," he said shortly, then decided there was no reason to bark at her because he was having trouble dealing with her. He looked at her. "I don't know people around here."

"See, you should," she said, tipping her head to one side to look at him. "You've lived here five years, Sam."

"I didn't move here for friends." He came to the mountains to find the peace that still eluded him.

"Doesn't mean you can't make some." Sighing, she turned her head to the flames. "If you did know people, you could help me on the puppy situation." Shaking her head, she added, "I've got her princess dolls and a fairy princess dress and the other small things she asked for. The puppy worries me."

He didn't want to think about children's Christmas dreams. Sam remembered another child dictating letters to Santa and waking to the splendor of Christmas morning. And through the pain he also recalled how he and his wife had worked to make those dreams come true for their little boy. So, though he hated it, he said, "You could get her a stuffed puppy with a note that Santa will bring her the real thing as soon as the puppy's ready for a new home."

She tipped her head to one side and studied him,

a wide smile on her face. God, when she smiled, her eyes shone and something inside him fisted into knots.

"A note from Santa himself? That's a good idea. I think Holly would love that he's going to make a special trip just for her." Clearly getting into it, she continued, "I could make up a certificate or something. You know—" she deepened her voice for dramatic effect "—*this is to certify that Holly Curran will be receiving a puppy from Santa as soon as the puppy is ready for a home*." Wrinkling her brow, she added thoughtfully, "Maybe I could draw a Christmas border on the paper and we could frame it for her—you know, with Santa's signature—and hang it in her bedroom. It could become an heirloom, something she passes down to her kids."

He shrugged, as if it meant nothing, but in his head, he could see Holly's excitement at a special visit from Santa *after* Christmas. But once December was done, he wouldn't be seeing Joy or Holly again, so he wouldn't know how the Santa promise went, would he? Frowning to himself, he tried to ignore the ripple of regret that swept through him.

"Okay, I am not responsible for your latest frown."

"What?" He turned his head to look at her again.

She laughed shortly. "Nothing. So, what'd you work on today?"

"Seriously?" Usually she just launched into a monologue.

"Well, you're actually speaking tonight," she said with a shrug, "so I thought I'd ask a question that wasn't rhetorical."

"Right." Shaking his head, he said, "I'm starting a new project."

"Another table?"

"No."

"Talking," she acknowledged, "but still far from chatty."

"Men are not chatty."

"Some men you can't shut up," she argued. "If it's not a table you're working on, what is it?"

"Haven't decided yet."

"You know, in theory, a job like that sounds wonderful." She took a sip of wine. "But I do better with a schedule all laid out in front of me. I like knowing that website updates are due on Monday and newsletters have to go out on Tuesday, like that."

"I don't like schedules."

She watched him carefully, and his internal radar went on alert. When a woman got that particular look in her eye—curiosity—it never ended well for a man.

"Well," she said softly, "if you haven't decided on a project yet, you could give me some help with the Santa certificate."

"What do you mean?" He heard the wariness in his own voice.

"I mean, you could draw Christmassy things around the borders, make it look beautiful." She

something because it seemed ridiculous to pretend I didn't know who you were."

He rubbed the heel of his hand at the center of his chest, trying to ease the ball of ice lodged there. "Fine. Don't pretend. Just ignore it."

"What good will that do?" She set her wine down on the table and stood up to face him. "I'm sorry but—"

"Don't. God, don't say you're sorry. I've had more than enough of that, thanks. I don't want your sympathy." He pushed one hand through his hair and felt the heat of the fire on his back.

This place had been his refuge. He'd buried his past back east and come here to get away from not only the press, but also the constant barrage of memories assaulting him at every familiar scene. He'd left his family because their pity had been thick enough to choke him. He'd left *himself* behind when he came to the mountains. The man he'd once been. The man who'd been so wrapped up in creating beauty that he hadn't noticed the beauty in his own life until it had been snatched away.

"Well, you've got it anyway," Joy told him and reached out to lay one hand on his forearm.

Her touch fired everything in him, heat erupting with a rush that jolted his body to life in a way he hadn't experienced in too many long, empty years. And he resented the hell out of it.

He pulled away from her, and his voice dripped

ice as he said, "Whatever it is you're after, you should know I don't want another woman in my life. Another child. Another loss."

Her gaze never left his, and those big blue pools of sympathy and irritation threatened to drown him.

"Everybody loses, Sam," she said quietly. "Houses, jobs, people they love. You can't insulate yourself from that. Protect yourself from pain. It's how you respond to the losses you experience that defines who you are."

He sneered at her. She had no idea. "And you don't like how I responded? Is that it? Well, get in line."

"Loss doesn't go away just because you're hiding from it."

Darkness beyond the windows seemed to creep closer, as if it were finding a way to slip right inside him. This room with its bright wood and soft lights and fire-lit shadows felt as if it were the last stand against the dark, and the light was losing.

Sam took a deep breath, looked down at her and said tightly, "You don't know what you're talking about."

Her head tipped to one side and blond curls fell against her neck. "You think you're the only one with pain?"

Of course not. But his own was too deep, too ingrained to allow him to give a flying damn what someone else might be suffering. "Just drop it. I'm done with this."

"Oh no. This you don't get to ignore. You think I don't know loss?" She moved in closer, tipped her head back and sent a steely-blue stare into his eyes. "My parents died when I was eight. I grew up in foster homes because I wasn't young enough or cute enough to be adopted."

"Damn it, Joy—" He'd seen pain reflected in his own eyes often enough to recognize the ghosts of it in hers. And he felt like the bastard he was for practically insisting that she dredge up her own past to do battle with his.

"As a foster kid I was never 'real' in any of the families I lived with. Always the outsider. Never fitting in. I didn't have friends, either, so I went out and made some."

"Good for you."

"Not finished. I had to build everything I have for myself *by* myself. I wanted to belong. I wanted family, you know?"

He started to speak, but she held up one hand for silence, and damned if it didn't work on him. He couldn't take his eyes off her as he watched her dip into the past to defend her present.

"I met Holly's father when I was designing his website. He was exciting and he loved me, and I thought it was forever—it lasted until I told him about Holly."

And though Sam felt bad, hearing it, watching it, knowing she'd had a tough time of it, he couldn't help but ask, "Yeah? Did he die? Did he take Holly away from you, so that you knew you'd never see her again?"

She huffed out a breath. "No, but—"

"Then you don't know," Sam interrupted, not caring now if he sounded like an unfeeling jerk. He wouldn't feel bad for the child she'd once been. *She* was the one who had dragged the ugly past into the present. "You can't possibly *know*, and I'm not going to stand here defending myself and my choices to you."

"Great," she said, nodding sharply as her temper once again rose to meet his. "So you'll just keep hiding yourself away until the rest of your life slides past?"

Sam snapped, throwing both hands high. "Why the hell do you care if I do?"

"Because I *saw* you with Holly," Joy said, moving in on him again, flavoring every breath he took with the scent of summer flowers that clung to her. "I saw your kindness. She needed that. Needs a male role model in her life and—"

"Oh, stop. Role models. For God's sake, I'm no one's father figure."

"Really?" She jammed both hands on her hips. "Better to shut yourself down? Pretend you're alone on a rock somewhere?"

"For me, yeah."

"You're lying."

"You don't know me."

"You'd like to think so," Joy said. "But you're not that hard to read, Sam."

Sam shook his head. "You're here to run the house, not psychoanalyze me."

"Multitasker, remember?" She smiled and he resented her for it. Resented knowing that he wanted her in spite of the tempers spiking between them. Hell, maybe *because* of it. He hated knowing that maybe she had a point. He really hated realizing that whatever secrets he thought he'd been keeping were no more private than the closest computer with an internet connection.

And man, it bugged him that she could go from anger to smiles in a blink.

"This isn't analysis, Sam." She met his gaze coolly, steadily, firelight dancing in her eyes. "It's called conversation."

"It's called my *family*," he said tightly, watching the reflection of flame and shadow in the blue of her eyes.

"I know. And—"

"Don't say you're sorry."

"I have to," she said simply. "And I am."

"Great. Thanks." God he wanted to get out of there. She was too close to him. He could smell her shampoo and the scent of flowers—Jasmine? Lilies?—fired a bolt of desire through him.

"But that's not all I am," she continued. "I'm also a little furious at you."

"Yeah? Right back at you."

"Good," she said, surprising him. "If you're angry at least you're *feeling* something." She moved in closer, kept her gaze locked with his and said, "If you love making furniture and working with wood, great. You're really good at it."

He nodded, hardly listening, his gaze shifting to the open doorway across the room. It—and the chance of escape—seemed miles away.

"But you shouldn't stop painting," she added fiercely. "The worlds you created were beautiful. Magical."

That magic was gone now, and it was better that way, he assured himself. But Sam couldn't remember a time when anyone had talked to him like this. Forcing him to remember. To face the darkness. To face himself. One reason he'd moved so far from his parents, his sister, was that they had been so careful. So cautious in everything they'd said as if they were all walking a tightrope, afraid to make the wrong move, say the wrong thing.

Their…*caution* had been like knives, jabbing at him constantly. Creating tiny nicks that festered and ached with every passing minute. So he'd moved here, where no one knew him. Where no one would offer sympathy he didn't want or advice he wouldn't take. He'd never counted on Joy.

"Why?" she asked. "Why would you give that up?"

It had been personal. So deeply personal he'd never talked about it with anyone, and he wasn't about to start now. Chest tight, mouth dry, he looked at her and said, "I'm not talking about this with you."

With anyone.

He took a step or two away from her, then spun back and around to glare down at her. In spite of the quick burst of fury inside him, sizzling around and between them, she didn't seem the least bit intimidated. Another thing to admire about her, damn it. She was sure of herself even when she was wrong.

"I already told you, Sam. You don't scare me."

"That's a damn shame," he muttered, trying not to remember that his mother had warned him about lonely old recluses muttering to themselves. He turned from her again, and this time she reached out and grabbed his arm as he moved away from her.

"Just stop," she demanded. "Stop and talk to me."

He glanced down at her hand on his arm and tried not to relish the heat sliding from her body into his. Tried not to notice that every cell inside him was waking up with a jolt. "Already told you I'm not talking about this."

"Then don't. Just stay. Talk to me." She took a deep breath, gave his arm a squeeze, then let him go. "Look, I didn't mean to bring any of this up tonight."

"Then why the hell did you?" He felt the loss of her touch and wanted it back.

"I don't like lying."

Scowling now, he asked, "What's that got to do with anything?"

Joy folded both arms in front of her and unconsciously lifted them until his gaze couldn't keep from admiring the pull of her shirt and the curve of those breasts. He shook his head and attempted to focus when she started talking again.

"I found out today about your family and not saying something would have felt like I was lying to you."

Convoluted, but in a weird way, she made sense. He wasn't much for lies, either, except for the ones he told his mother every time he assured her that he was fine. And truth be told, he would have been fine with Joy pretending she knew nothing about his past. But it was too late now for pretense.

"Okay, great. Conscience clear. Now let's move on." He started walking again and this time, when Joy tugged on his arm to get him to stop, he whirled around to face her.

Her blue eyes went wide, her mouth opened and he pulled her into him. It was instinct, pure, raw instinct, that had him grabbing her close. He speared his fingers through those blond curls, pulled her head back and kissed her with all the pent-up frustration, desire and, yeah, even temper that was clawing at him.

Surprised, it took her only a second or two to react. Joy wrapped her arms around his waist and moved in even closer. Sam's head exploded at the first, incredible taste of her. And then he wanted more. A groan slid from her throat, and that sound fed the flames enveloping him. God, he'd had no idea what kissing her would do to him. He'd been thinking about this for days, and having her in his arms made him want the feel of her skin beneath his hands. The heat of her body surrounding his.

All he could think was to get her clothes off her. To cup her breasts, to take each of her nipples into his mouth and listen to the whimpering sounds of pleasure she would make as he took her. He wanted to look down into blue eyes and watch them go blind with passion. He wanted to feel her hands sliding across his skin, holding him tightly to her.

His kiss deepened farther, his tongue tangling with hers in a frenzied dance of desire that pumped through him with the force and rush of a wildfire screaming across the hillsides.

Joy clung to him, letting him know in the most primal way that she felt the same. That her own needs and desires were pushing at her. He took her deeper, held her tighter and spun her around toward the closest couch. Heart pounding, breath slamming in and out of his lungs, he kept his mouth fused to hers as he laid her down on the wide, soft cushions and followed after, keeping her close to his side. She arched up, back bowing as he ran one hand up and down the length of her. All he could think about was touching her skin, feeling the heat of her. He flipped the button of her jeans open, pulled down the zipper, then slid his hand down, across her abdomen, feeling her shiver with every inch of flesh he claimed. His fingers slipped beneath the band of her panties and she lifted her hips as he moved to cup her heat.

She gasped, tore her mouth from his and clutched at his shoulders when he stroked her for the first time. He loved the feel of her—slick, wet, hot. His body tightened painfully as he stared into her eyes. His mind fuzzed out and his body ached. He touched her, again and again, stroking, pushing into her heat, caressing her inside and out, driving them both to the edge of insanity.

"Sam—" She breathed his name and that soft, whispered sound rattled him.

When had she become so important? When had touching her become imperative? He took her mouth, tangling his tongue with hers, taking the taste of her deep inside him as he felt her body coil tighter with the need swamping her. She rocked into his hand, her hips pumping as he pushed her higher, faster. He pulled his head back, wanting, needing to see her eyes glaze with passion when the orgasm hit her.

He wasn't disappointed. She jolted in his arms when his thumb stroked across that one small nub of sensation at the heart of her. Everything she was feeling flashed through her eyes, across her features. He was caught up, unable to tear his gaze from hers. Joy

Curran was a surprise to him on so many levels, he felt as though he'd never really learn them all. And at the moment, he didn't have to. Right now, he wanted only to hold her as she shattered.

She called his name again and he clutched her to him as her body trembled and shivered in his grasp. Her climax rolled on and on, leaving her breathless and Sam more needy than ever.

His body ached to join hers. His heart pounded in a fast gallop that left him damn near shaking with the want clawing at him.

"Sam," she whispered, reaching up to cup his face with her palms. "Sam, I need—"

He knew just what she needed because he needed it too. He shifted, pulled his hand free of her body and thought only about stripping them both out of their clothes.

In one small, rational corner of his mind, Sam admitted to himself that he'd never known anything like this before. This pulsing, blinding, overpowering sense of need and pleasure and craving to be part of a woman. To be locked inside her body and lose himself in her. Never.

Not even with Dani.

That thought broke him. He pulled back abruptly and stared down at Joy like a blind man seeing the light for the first time. Both exhilarated and terrified. A bucket full of ice water dumped on his head wouldn't have shocked him more.

He fought for breath, for balance, but there wasn't any to be had. His own mind was shouting at him, telling him he was a bastard for feeling more for Joy than he had for his wife. Telling him to deny it, even to himself. To bury these new emotions and go back to feeling nothing. It was safer.

"That's it," he said, shaking his head, rolling off the couch, then taking a step, then another, away from her. "I can't do this."

"Sure you can," Joy assured him, a confused half smile on her face as her breath came in short, hard gasps. She pushed herself up to her elbows on the couch. Her hair was a wild tumble of curls and her jeans still lay open, invitingly. "You were doing great."

"I *won't* do this." His eyes narrowed on her. "Not again."

"Sam, we should talk—"

He actually laughed, though to him it sounded harsh, strained as it scraped against his throat. "Talking doesn't solve everything and it won't solve this. I'm going out to the workshop."

Joy watched him go, her lips still buzzing from that kiss. Her heart still pounding like a bass drum. She might even have gone after him if her legs weren't trembling so badly she was forced to drop into the closest chair.

What the hell had just happened?

And how could she make it happen again?

Seven

Joy didn't see Sam at all the next morning, and maybe that was just as well.

She'd lain awake most of the night, reliving the whole scene, though she could admit to herself she spent more time reliving the kiss and the feel of his amazingly talented fingers on her body than the argument that had prompted it. Even now, though, she cringed a little remembering how she'd thrown the truth of his past at him out of nowhere. Honestly, what had she been thinking, just blurting out the fact that she knew about his family? She hadn't been thinking at all—that was the problem.

She'd stared into those amazing eyes of his and had seen him shuttered away, closing himself off, and it had just made her so angry, she'd confronted him without considering what it might do to the tenuous relationship they already had.

In Kaye's two-bedroom suite off the kitchen, there had been quiet in Joy's room and innocent dreams in Holly's. The house seemed to sigh with a cold wind that whipped through the pines and rattled glass panes. And Joy hadn't been able to shut off her brain. Or her body. But once she'd gotten past the buzz running rampant through her veins, all she'd been able to think about was the look in his eyes when she'd brought up his lost family.

Lying there in the dark, she'd assured herself that once she'd said the words, opened a door into his past, there'd been no going back. She could still see the shock in his eyes when she'd brought it up, and a twinge of guilt wrapped itself around her heart. But it was no match for the ribbon of anger that was there as well.

Not only had he walked away from his talent, but he'd shut himself off from life. From any kind of future or happiness. Why? His suffering wouldn't bring them back. Wouldn't restore the family he'd lost.

"Mommy, are you all done now?"

Joy came out of her thoughts and looked at her daughter, beside her at the kitchen table. Behind them, the outside world was gray and the pines bent nearly in half from that wind sweeping in off the lake.

Still no snow and Joy was beginning to think they wouldn't have a white Christmas after all.

But for now, in the golden lamplight, she looked at Holly, doing her alphabet and numbers on her electronic tablet. The little girl was squirming in her seat, clearly ready to be done with the whole sit-down-and-work thing.

"Not yet, baby," Joy said, and knew that if her brain hadn't been filled with images of Sam, she'd have been finished with the website update a half hour ago. But no, all she could think of was the firelight in his eyes. The taste of his mouth. The feel of his hard body pressed to hers. And the slick glide of his fingers.

Oh, boy.

"Almost, honey," she said, clearing her throat and focusing again on the comments section of her client's website. For some reason people who read books felt it was okay to go on the author's website and list the many ways the author could have made the book better. Even when they loved it, they managed to sneak in a couple of jabs. It was part of Joy's job to remove the comments that went above and beyond a review and deep into the realm of harsh criticism.

"Mommy," Holly said, her heels kicking against the rungs of the kitchen chair, "when can we gooooooo?"

A one-syllable word now six syllables.

"As soon as I'm finished, sweetie," Joy promised,

focusing on her laptop screen rather than the never-ending loop of her time with Sam. Once the comment section was cleaned up, Joy posted her client's holiday letter to her fans, then closed up the site and opened the next one.

Another holiday letter to post and a few pictures the author had taken at the latest writers' conference she'd attended.

"How much longer, though?" Holly asked, just a touch of a wheedling whine in her voice. "If we don't go soon all the Christmas trees will be *gone*."

Drama, thy name is Holly, Joy thought with a smile. Reaching out, she gave one of the girl's pigtails a tug. "Promise, there will be lots of trees when we get into town. But remember, we're getting a little one this year, okay?" Because of the Grinch and his aversion to all things festive.

"I know! It's like a fairy tree cuz it's tiny and can go on a table to put in our room cuz Sam doesn't like Christmas." Her head tipped to one side. "How come he doesn't, Mommy? Everybody likes presents."

"I don't know, baby." She wasn't about to try to explain Sam's penchant for burying himself in a love-less, emotionless well. "You should ask him some-time."

"I'll ask him now!" She scrambled off her chair and Joy thought about calling her back as she raced to get her jacket. But why should she? Joy had already seen Sam with Holly. He was kind. Patient. And she knew darn well that even if the man was furious with *her*, he wouldn't take it out on Holly.

And maybe it would be good for him to be faced with all that cheerful optimism. All that innocence shining around her girl.

In seconds, Holly was back, dancing in place on the toes of her pink princess sneakers. Joy zipped up the jacket, pulled up Holly's hood and tied it at the neck. Then she took a moment to just look at the little girl who was really the light of her life. Love welled up inside her, thick and rich, and she heard Sam's voice in her mind again.

Did he take Holly away from you, so that you knew you'd never see her again?

That thought had Joy grabbing her daughter and pulling her in close for a tight hug that had Holly wriggling for freedom. He was right, she couldn't really *know* what he'd survived. She didn't even want to imagine it.

"You're squishing me, Mommy!"

"Sorry, baby." She swallowed the knot in her throat and gave her girl a smile. "You go ahead and play with Sam. I'll come get you when it's time to go. As soon as I finish doing the updates on this website. Promise."

"Okay!" Holly turned to go and stopped when Joy spoke up again.

"No wandering off, Holly. Right to the workshop."

"Can't I look at my fairy house Sam helped me make? There might be fairies there now."

Boy, she was really going to miss this imaginative age when Holly grew out of it. But, though the fairy house wasn't exactly *inside* the woods, it was close enough that a little girl might be tempted to walk in more deeply and then end up getting lost. So, no. "We'll look later."

"Okay, 'bye!" And she was gone like a tiny pink hurricane.

Joy glanced out the window and watched her daughter bullet across the lawn to the workshop and then slip inside the doors. Smiling to herself, she thought she'd give a lot to see Sam's reaction to his visitor.

"Hi, Sam! Mommy said I could come play with you!"

She didn't catch him completely by surprise. Thankfully, Sam had spotted the girl running across the yard and had had time to toss a heavy beige tarp over his latest project. Although why he'd started on it was beyond him. A whim that had come on him two days ago, he'd thrown himself into it late last night when he'd left Joy in the great room.

Guilt had pushed him away from her, and it was guilt that had kept him working half the night. Memories crowded his brain, but it was thoughts of Joy herself that kept him on edge. That kiss. The heavy sigh of her breath as she molded herself to him. The eager response and matching need that had thrown him harder than he'd expected.

Shaking his head, he grumbled, "Don't have time to play." He turned to his workbench to find *something* to do.

"I can help you like I did with the fairy house. I want to see if there are fairies there but Mommy said I couldn't go by myself. Do you want to go with me? Cuz we can be busy outside, too, can't we?" She walked farther into the room and, as if she had radar, moved straight to the tarp draped across his project. "What's this?"

"Mine," he said and winced at the sharpness of his tone. But the girl, just like her mother, was impossible to deflate. She simply turned that bright smile of hers on him and said, "It's a secret, right? I like secrets. I can tell you one. It's about Lizzie's mommy going to have another baby. She thinks Lizzie doesn't know but Lizzie heard her mommy tell her daddy that she passed the test."

Too much information coming too quickly. He'd already learned about the wonderful Lizzie and her puppy. And this latest news blast might come under the heading of TMI.

"I wanted a sister, too," Holly said and walked right up to his workbench, climbing onto the stool she'd used the last time she was there. "But Mommy says I have to have a puppy instead and that's all right cuz babies cry a lot and a puppy doesn't…"

"Why don't we go check the fairy house?" Sam said, interrupting the flow before his head exploded. Getting her out of the shop seemed the best way to keep her from asking about the tarp again. It wasn't as if he *wanted* to go look for fairies in the freezing-cold woods.

"Oh, boy!" She squirmed off the stool, then grabbed his hand with her much smaller one.

Just for a second, Sam felt a sharp tug at the edges of his heart, and it was painful. Holly was older than Eli had been, he told himself, and she was a girl—so completely different children. But he couldn't help wondering what Eli would have been like at Holly's age. Or as he would be now at almost nine. But Eli would always be three years old. Just finding himself. Just becoming more of a boy than a baby and never a chance to be more.

"Let's go, Sam!" Holly pulled on his hand and leaned forward as if she could drag him behind her if she just tried hard enough.

He folded his fingers around hers and let her lead him from the shop into the cold. And he listened to her talk, heard again about puppies and fairies and princesses, and told himself that maybe this was his punishment. Being lulled into affection for a child who wasn't his. A child who would disappear from his life in a few short weeks.

And he wasn't completely stupid, he told himself. He could see through Joy's machinations. She wanted to wake him up, she'd said. To drag him back into the land of the living, and clearly, she was allowing her daughter to be part of that program.

"There it is!" Holly's excitement ratcheted up another level, and Sam thought the girl's voice hit a pitch that only dogs should have been able to hear. But her absolute pleasure in the smallest things was hard to ignore, damn it.

She let go of his hand and ran the last few steps to the fairy house on her own. Bending down, she inspected every window and even opened the tiny door to look inside. And Sam was drawn to the girl's absolute faith that she would see *something*. Even disappointment didn't jar the thrill in her eyes. "I don't see them," she said, turning her head to look at him.

"Maybe they're out having a picnic," he said, surprising himself by playing into the game. "Or shopping."

"Like Mommy and me are gonna do," Holly said, jumping up and down as if she simply couldn't hold back the excitement any more. "We're gonna get a Christmas tree today."

He felt a hitch in the center of his chest, but he didn't say anything.

"We're getting a little one this time to put in our room cuz you don't like Christmas. How come you don't like Christmas, Sam?"

"I…it's complicated." He hunched deeper into his black leather jacket and stuffed both hands into the pockets.

"Compulcated?"

"Complicated," he corrected, wondering how the hell he'd gotten into this conversation with a five-year-old.

"Why?"

"Because it's about a lot of things all at once," he said, hoping to God she'd leave it there. He should have known better.

Her tiny brow furrowed as she thought about it. Finally, though, she shrugged and said, "Okay. Do you think fairies go buy Christmas trees? Will there be lights in their little house? Can I see 'em?"

So grateful to have left the Christmas thing behind, he said, "Maybe if you look really hard one night you'll see some."

"I can look *really* hard, see?" Her eyes squinted and her mouth puckered up, showing him just how strong her looking power was.

"That's pretty hard." The wind gave a great gust and about knocked Holly right off her feet. He reached out, steadied her, then said, "You should go on back to the house with your mom."

"But we're not done looking." She grabbed his hand again, and this time, it was more comforting than unsettling. Pulling on him, she wandered over to one side of the fairy house, where the pine needles lay thick as carpet on the ground. "Could we make another fairy house and put it right here, by this big tree? That's like a Christmas tree, right? Maybe the fairies would put lights on it, too."

He was scrambling now. He'd never meant to get so involved. Not with the child. Not with her mother. But Holly's sweetness and Joy's...*everything*...kept sucking him in. Now he was making fairy houses and secret projects and freezing his ass off looking for invisible creatures.

"Sure," he said, in an attempt to get the girl moving toward the house. "We can build another one. In a day or two. Maybe."

"Okay, tomorrow we can do it and put it by the tree and the fairies will have a Christmas house to be all nice and warm. Can we put blankets and stuff in there, too?"

Tomorrow. Just like her mother, Holly heard only what she wanted to hear and completely disregarded everything else. He glanced at the house and somehow wasn't surprised to see Joy in the kitchen window, watching them. Across the yard, their gazes met and heat lit up the line of tension linking them.

All he could think of was the taste of her. The feel of her. The gnawing realization that he was going to have her. There was no mistaking the pulse-pounding sensations linking them. No pretending that it wasn't there. Guilt still chewing at him, he knew that even that wouldn't be enough to keep him from her.

And when she lifted one hand and laid it palm flat on the window glass, it was as if she was touching him. Feeling what he was feeling and acknowledging that she, too, knew the inevitable was headed right at them.

The trunk was filled with grocery bags, the backseat held a Charlie Brown Christmas tree on one side and Holly on the other, and now, Joy was at her house for the boxes of decorations they would need.

"Our house is tiny, huh, Mommy?"

After Sam's house, *anything* would look tiny, but in this case especially. "Sure is, baby," she said, "but it's ours."

She noted Buddy Hall's shop van in the driveway and hurriedly got Holly out of the car and hustling toward the house. Funny, she'd never really noticed before that they didn't have many trees on their street, Joy thought. But spending the last week or so at Sam's house—surrounded by the woods and a view of the lake—she couldn't help thinking that her street looked a little bare. But it wasn't Sam's house that intrigued her. It was the man himself. Instantly, she thought of the look he'd given her just that morning. Even from across the wide yard, she'd felt the power of that stare, and her blood had buzzed in reaction. Even now, her stomach jumped with nerves and expectation. She and Sam weren't finished. Not by a long shot. There was more coming. She just wasn't sure what or when. But she couldn't wait.

"Stay with me, sweetie," Joy said as they walked into the house together.

"Okay. Can I have a baby sister?"

Joy stopped dead on the threshold and looked down at her. "What? Where did that come from?"

"Lizzie's getting a new sister. It's a secret but she is and I want one, too."

Deb was pregnant? Why hadn't she told? And how the heck did Holly know before Joy did? Shaking her head, she told herself they were all excellent questions that would have to be answered later. For now, she wanted to check on the progress of the house repairs.

"Buddy?" she called out.

"Back here." The deep voice came from the kitchen, so Joy kept a grip on Holly and headed that way.

Along the way, her mind kept up a constant comparison between her own tiny rental and the splendor of Sam's place. The hallway alone was a fraction of the length of his. The living room was so small that if four people were in there at the same time, they'd be in sin. The kitchen, she thought sadly, walking into the room, looked about as big as the island in Sam's kitchen. Its sad cabinets needed paint and really just needed to be torn down and replaced, but since she was just a renter, it wasn't up to her. And the house might be small and a little on the shabby side, but it was her home. The one she'd made for her and Holly, so there was affection along with the exasperation.

"How's it going, Buddy?" she asked.

"Not bad." He stood up, all five feet four inches of him, with his barrel chest and broader stomach. A gray fringe of hair haloed his head, and his bright blue eyes sparkled with good humor. "Just sent Buddy Junior down to the hardware store. Thought while I was here we could fix the hinges on some of these cabinets. Some of 'em hang so crooked they're making me dizzy."

Delighted, Joy said, "Thank you, Buddy. That's going the extra mile."

"Not a problem." He pushed up the sleeves of his flannel shirt, took a step back and looked at the gaping hole where a light switch used to be. "Got the wiring all replaced and brought up to code out in the living room, but I'm checking the rest, as well. You've got some fraying in here and a hot wire somebody left uncapped in the smaller bedroom—"

Holly's bedroom, Joy thought and felt a pang of worry. God, if the fire had started in her daughter's room in the middle of the night, maybe they wouldn't have noticed in time. Maybe smoke inhalation would have knocked them out and kept them out until—

"No worries," Buddy said, looking right at her. "No point in thinking about what-ifs, either," he added as if he could look at her and read her thoughts. And he probably could. "By the time this job's done I guarantee all the wiring. You and the little one there will be safe as houses."

"What's a safe house?" Holly asked.

Buddy winked at her. "This one, soon's I'm done."

"Thank you, Buddy. I really appreciate it." But maybe, Joy told herself, it was time to find a new house for her and her daughter. Something newer. Safer. Still, that was a thought for later on, so she put it aside for now.

"I know you do and we're getting it done as fast as we can." He gave his own work a long look. "The way it's looking, you could be back home before Christmas."

Back home. Away from Sam. Away from what she was beginning to feel for him. Probably best, she told herself, though right at the moment, she didn't quite believe it. As irritating as the man could be, he was so much more. And that more was drawing her in.

"Appreciate that, too," Joy said. "We're just here to pick up some Christmas decorations, then we'll get out of your hair."

He grinned and scrubbed one hand across the top of his bald head. "You'd have quite the time getting *in* my hair. You two doing all right up the mountain?"

"Yes." Everyone in town was curious about Sam, she thought. Didn't he see that if he spent more time talking to people they'd be less inclined to talk about him and wonder? "It's been great. Sam helped Holly build a fairy house."

"Is that right?"

"It's pretty and in the woods and I'm going to bring some of my dolls to put in it to keep the fairies company and Sam's gonna help me make another one, too. He's really nice. Just crabby sometimes."

"Out of the mouths of babes," Joy murmured with a smile. "Well, we've got to run. Trees to decorate, cookies to bake."

"You go ahead then," Buddy said, already turning back to his task. Then over his shoulder he called out, "You be sure to tell Sam Henry my wife, Cora, loves that rocking chair he made. She bought it at Crafty and now I can't hardly get her out of it."

Joy smiled. "I'll tell him."

Then with Holly rummaging through her toys, Joy bundled up everything Christmas. A few minutes later, they were back in the car, and she was thinking about the crabby man who made her want things she shouldn't.

Of course, she had to stop by Deb's first, because hello, *news*. "Why didn't you tell me you're pregnant?"

Deb's eyes went wide and when her jaw dropped she popped a mini apple pie into it. "How did you know?"

"Lizzie told Holly, Holly told me."

"Lizzie—" Deb sighed and shook her head. "You

think your kids don't notice what's going on. Boy, I'm going to have to get better at the secret thing."

"Why a secret?" Joy picked up a tiny brownie and told herself the calories didn't count since it was so small. Drawing it out into two bites, she waited.

"You know we lost one a couple of years ago," Deb said, keeping her voice low as there were customers in the main room, separated from them only by the swinging door between the kitchen and the store's front.

"Yeah." Joy reached out and gave her friend a sympathetic pat on the arm.

"Well, this time we didn't want to tell anyone until we're at least three months. You know?" She sighed again and gave a rueful smile. "But now that Lizzie's spreading the word…"

"Bag open, cat out," Joy said, grinning. "This is fabulous. I'm happy for you."

"Thanks. Me, too."

"Of course, now Holly wants a baby, too."

Deb gave her a sly look. "You could do something about that, you know."

"Right. Because I'm such a great single mom I should do it again."

"You are and it wouldn't kill you," Deb told her, "but I was thinking more along the lines of gorgeous hermit slash painter slash craftsman."

"Yeah, I don't think so." Of course, she immediately thought of that kiss and the tension that had been coiled in her middle all day. Briefly, her brain skipped to hazy images of her and Sam and Holly living in that big beautiful house together. With a couple more babies running around and a life filled with hot kisses, warm laughter and lots of love.

But fantasies weren't real life, and she'd learned long ago to concentrate on what was real. Otherwise, building dreams on boggy ground could crush your heart. Yes, she cared about Sam. But he'd made it clear he wasn't interested beyond stoking whatever blaze was burning between them. And yet, she thought, brain still racing, he was so good with Holly. And Joy's little girl was blossoming, having a man like Sam pay attention to her. Spend time with her.

Okay, her mind warned sternly, *dial it back now, Joy. No point in setting yourself up for that crush.*

"You say no, but your eyes are saying yum." Deb filled a tray with apple pies no bigger than silver dollars, laying them all out on paper doilies that made them look like loosely wrapped presents.

"Yum is easy—it's what comes after that's hard."

"Since when are you afraid of hard work?"

"I'm not, but—" Not the same thing, she told herself, as working to make a living, to build a life. This was bringing a man out of the shadows, and what if once he was out he didn't want her anyway? No, that way lay pain and misery, and why should she set herself up for that?

"You're alone, he's alone, match made in heaven."

"Alone isn't a good enough reason for anyone, Deb." She stopped, snatched another brownie and asked, "When did this get to be about me instead of you?"

"Since I hate seeing my best friend—a completely wonderful human being—all by herself."

"I'm not alone. I have Holly."

"And I love her, too, but it's not the same and you know it."

Slumping, Joy leaned one hip against the counter and nibbled at her second brownie. "No, it's not. And okay, fine—I'm...intrigued by Sam."

"Intrigued is good. Sex is better."

Sadly, she admitted, "I wouldn't know."

"Yeah, that would be my point."

"It's not that easy," Joy said wistfully. Then she glanced out the window at the house across the yard where Holly and Lizzie were probably driving Sean Casey insane about now. "I mean, he's—and I'm—"

"Something happened."

Her gaze snapped to Deb's. "Just a kiss."

"Yay. And?"

"And," Joy admitted, "then he got a little more involved and completely melted my underwear."

"Wow." Deb gave a sigh and fluttered one hand over her heart.

"Yeah. We were arguing and we were both furious and he kissed me and—" she slapped her hands together "—boom."

"Oh, boom is good."

"It's great, but it doesn't solve anything."

"Honey," Deb asked with a shake of her head, "who cares?"

Joy laughed. Honestly, Deb was really good for her. "Okay, I'm heading back to the house. Even when it's this cold outside, I shouldn't be leaving the groceries in the car this long."

"Fine, but I'm going to want to hear more about this 'boom.'"

"Yeah," Joy said, "me, too. So are the girls still on for the sleepover?"

"Are you kidding? Lizzie's been planning this for days. Popcorn, princess movies and s'mores cooked over the fireplace."

Ordinarily, Holly would be too young for a sleepover, but Joy knew Deb was as crazy protective as she was. "Okay, then I'll bring her to your house Saturday afternoon."

"Don't forget to pray for me," Deb said with a smile. "Two five-year-olds for a night filled with squeals…"

"You bet."

"And take that box of brownies with you. Sweeten up your hermit and maybe there'll be more 'boom.'"

"I don't know about that, but I will definitely take the brownies." When she left the warm kitchen, she paused on the back porch and tipped her face up to the gray sky. As she stood there, snow drifted lazily down and kissed her heated cheeks with ice.

Maybe it would be enough to cool her off, she told herself, crossing the yard to Deb's house to collect Holly and head home. But even as she thought it, Joy realized that nothing was going to cool her off as long as her mind was filled with thoughts of Sam.

Eight

Once it started snowing, it just kept coming. As if an invisible hand had pulled a zipper on the gray, threatening clouds, they spilled down heavy white flakes for days. The woods looked magical, and every day, Holly insisted on checking the fairy houses—there were now two—to see if she could catch a glimpse of the tiny people living in them. Every day there was disappointment, but her faith never wavered.

Sam had to admire that even as his once-cold heart warmed with affection for the girl. She was getting to him every bit as much as her mother was. In different ways, of course, but the result was the same. He was opening up, and damned if it wasn't painful as all hell. Every time that ice around his heart cracked a little more, and with it came the pain that reminded him why the ice had been there in the first place.

He was on dangerous ground, and there didn't seem to be a way to back off. Coming out of the shadows could blind a man if he wasn't careful. And that was one thing Sam definitely was.

Once upon a time, things had been different. *He* had been different. He'd gone through life thinking nothing could go wrong. Though at the time, everywhere he turned, things went his way so he couldn't really be blamed for figuring it would always be like that.

His talent had pushed him higher in the art world than he'd ever believed possible, but it was his own ego that had convinced him to believe every accolade given. He'd thought of himself as blessed. As *chosen* for greatness. And looking back now, he could almost laugh at the deluded man he'd been.

Almost. Because when he'd finally had his ass handed to him, it had knocked the world out from under his feet. Feeling bulletproof only made recovering from a crash that much harder. And he couldn't even really say he'd recovered. He'd just marched on, getting by, getting through. What happened to his family wasn't something you ever got *over*. The most you could do was keep putting one foot in front of the other and hope that eventually you got somewhere.

Of course, he'd gotten *here*. To this mountain with

the beautiful home he shared with a housekeeper he paid to be there. To solitude that sometimes felt like a noose around his neck. To cutting ties to his family because he couldn't bear their grief as well as his own.

He gulped down a swallow of hot coffee and relished the burn. He stared out the shop window at the relentless snow and listened to the otherworldly quiet that those millions of falling flakes brought. In the quiet, his mind turned to the last few days. To Joy. The tension between them was strung as tight as barbed wire and felt just as lethal. Every night at dinner, he sat at the table with her and her daughter and pretended his insides weren't churning. Every night, he avoided meeting up with Joy in the great room by locking himself in the shop to work on what was under that tarp. And finally, he lay awake in his bed wishing to hell she was lying next to him.

He was a man torn by too many things. Too twisted around on the road he'd been walking for so long to know which way to head next. So he stayed put. In the shop. Alone.

Across the yard the kitchen light sliced into the dimness of the gray morning when Holly jerked the door open and stepped outside. He watched her and wasn't disappointed by her shriek of excitement. The little girl turned back to the house, shouted something to her mother and waited, bouncing on her toes until Joy joined her at the door. Holly pointed across the yard toward the trees and, with a wide grin on her face, raced down the steps and across the snow-covered ground.

Her pink jacket and pink boots were like hope in the gray, and Sam smiled to himself, wondering when he'd fallen for the kid. When putting up with her had become caring for her. When he'd loosened up enough to make a tiny dream come true.

Sam was already outside when Holly raced toward him in a wild flurry of exhilaration. He smiled at the shine in her eyes, at the grin that lit up her little face like a sunbeam. Then she threw herself at him, hugging his legs, throwing her head back to look up at him.

"Sam! Sam! Did you see?" Her words tumbled over each other in the rush to share her news. She grabbed his hand and tugged, her pink gloves warm against his fingers. "Come on! Come on! You have to see! They came! They came! I knew they would. I knew it and now they're here!"

Snow fell all around them, dusting Holly's jacket hood and swirling around Joy as she waited, her gaze fixed on his. And suddenly, all he could see were those blue eyes of hers, filled with emotion. A long, fraught moment passed between them before Holly's insistence shattered it. "Look, Sam. Look!"

She tugged him down on the ground beside her, then threw her arms around his neck and held on tight. Practically vibrating with excitement, Holly gave him a loud, smacking kiss on the cheek, then pulled back and looked at him with wonder in her eyes. "They came, Sam. They're living in our houses!"

Still reeling from that freely given hug and burst of affection, Sam stood up on unsteady legs. Smiling down at the little girl as she crawled around the front of the houses, peering into windows that shone with tiny Christmas lights, he felt another chunk of ice drop away from his heart. In the gray of the day, those bright specks of blue, green, red and yellow glittered like magic. Which was, he told himself, what Holly saw as she searched in vain to catch a glimpse of the fairies themselves.

He glanced at Joy again and she was smiling, a soft, knowing curve of her mouth that gleamed in her eyes, as well. There was something else in her gaze, too—beyond warmth, even beyond heat, and he wondered about it while Holly spun long, intricate stories about the fairies who lived in the tiny houses in the woods.

"You didn't have to do this," Joy said for the tenth time in a half hour.

"I'm gonna have popcorn with Lizzie and watch the princess movie," Holly called out from the backseat.

"Good for you," Sam said with a quick glance into the rearview mirror. Holly was looking out the side window, watching the snow and making her plans.

He looked briefly to Joy. "How else were you going to get into town?"

"I could have called Deb, asked her or Sean to come and pick up Holly."

"Right, or we could do it the easy way and have me drive you both in." Sam kept his gaze on the road. The snow was falling, not really heavy yet, but determined. It was already piling up on the side of the road, and he didn't even want to think about Joy and Holly, alone in a car, maneuvering through the storm that would probably get worse. A few minutes later, he pulled up outside the Casey house and was completely stunned when, sprung from her car seat, Holly leaned over and kissed his cheek. "'Bye, Sam!"

It was the second time he'd been on the receiving end of a simple, cheerfully given slice of affection that day, and again, Sam was touched more deeply than he wanted to admit. Shaken, he watched Joy walk Holly to her friend's house and waited until she came back, alone, and slid into the car beside him.

"She hardly paused long enough to say goodbye to me." Joy laughed a little. "She's been excited by the sleepover for days, but now the fairy houses are the big story." She clicked her seat belt into place, then turned to face him. "She was telling Lizzie all about the lights in the woods and promising that you and she will make Lizzie a fairy house, too."

"Great," he said, shaking his head as he backed out of the driveway. He wasn't sure how he'd been sucked into the middle of Joy's and Holly's lives, but here he was, and he had to admit—though he didn't like to—that he was *enjoying* it. Honestly, it worried him a little just how much he enjoyed it.

He liked hearing them in his house. Liked Holly popping in and out of the workshop, sharing dinner with them at the big dining room table. He even actually liked building magical houses for invisible beings. "More fairies."

"It's your own fault," she said, reaching out to lay one hand on his arm. "What you did was—it meant a lot. To Holly. To *me*."

The warmth of her touch seeped down into his bones and quickly spread throughout his body. Something else he liked. That jolt of heat when Joy was near. The constant ache of need that seemed to always be with him these days. He hadn't wanted a woman like this in years. He swallowed hard against the demand clawing at him and turned for the center of town and the road back to the house.

"We're not in a hurry, are we?" she asked.

Sam stopped at a red light and looked at her warily. "Why?"

"Because, it's early, but we could stay in town for a while. Have dinner at the steak house…"

She gave him a smile designed to bring a man to his knees. And it was working.

"You want to go out to dinner?" he asked.

"Well," she said, shrugging. "It's early, but that won't kill us."

He frowned and threw a glance out the windshield at the swirls of white drifting down from a leaden sky. "Still snowing. We should get up the mountain while we still can."

She laughed and God, he loved the sound of it— even if it was directed at him and his lame attempt to get out of town.

"It's not a blizzard, Sam. An hour won't hurt either of us."

"Easy for you to say," Sam muttered darkly. "You *like* talking to people." The sound of her laughter filled the truck and eased his irritation as he headed toward the restaurant.

Everybody in town had to be in the steak house, and Joy thought it was a good thing. She knew a lot of people in Franklin and she made sure to introduce Sam to most of them. Sure, it didn't make for a relaxing dinner—she could actually *see* him tightening up—but it felt good to watch people greet him. To tell him how much they loved the woodworking he did. And the more uncomfortable he got with the praise, the more Joy relished it.

He'd been too long in his comfort zone of solitude. He'd made himself an island, and swimming to the mainland would be exhausting. But it would so be worth the trip.

"I've never owned anything as beautiful as that bowl you made," Elinor Cummings gushed, laying one hand on Sam's shoulder in benediction. She was in her fifties, with graying black hair that had been ruthlessly sprayed into submission.

"Thanks." He shot Joy a look that promised payback in the very near future. She wasn't worried. Like an injured animal, Sam would snarl and growl at anyone who came too close. But he wouldn't bite.

"I love what you did with the bowl. The rough outside, looks as though you just picked it up off the forest floor—" Elinor continued.

"I did," Sam said, clearly hoping to cut her off, but pasting a polite, if strained, smile on his face.

"—and the inside looks like a jewel," she continued, undeterred from lavishing him with praise. "All of those lovely colors in the grain of that wood, all so polished, and it just gleams in the light." She planted one hand against her chest and gave a sigh. "It's simply lovely. Two sides of life," she mused, "that's what it says to me, two sides, the hard and the good, the sad and the glad. It's lovely. Just lovely."

"All right now, Ellie," her husband said, with an understanding wink for Sam and Joy, "let's let the man eat. Good to meet you, Sam."

Sam nodded, then reached for the beer in front of him and took a long pull. The Cummingses had been just the last in a long stream of people who'd stopped by their table to greet Joy and meet Sam. Every damn one of them had given him a look that said *Ah, the hermit. That's what he looks like!*

And then had come the speculative glances, as they wondered whether Sam and Joy were a couple, and that irritated him, as well. This was what happened when you met people. They started poking their noses into your life and pretty soon, that life was open season to anyone with a sense of curiosity. As the last of the strangers went back to their own tables, he glared at Joy.

"You're enjoying this, aren't you?"

In the light of the candle at their table, her eyes sparkled as she grinned. "I could try to deny it, but why bother? Yes, I am. It's good to see you actually forced to talk to people. And Elinor clearly loves your work. Isn't it nice to hear compliments?"

"It's a bowl." He sighed. "Nothing deep or meaningful to the design. Just a bowl. People always want to analyze, interpret what the artist meant. Sometimes a bowl is just a bowl."

She laughed and shook her head. "You can't fool me. I've seen your stuff in Crafty. Nothing about what you make is 'just' anything. People love your work, and if you gave them half a chance, they'd like you, too."

"And I want that because…"

"Because it's better than being a recluse." Joy leaned forward, bracing her elbows on the table. "Honestly, Sam, you can't stay on the mountain by yourself forever."

He hated admitting even to himself that she was right. Hell, he'd talked more, listened more, in the last couple of weeks than he had in years. His house wasn't empty. Wasn't filled with the careful quiet he normally knew. Kaye generally left him to his own devices, so he was essentially alone, even when his housekeeper was there. Joy and Holly had pushed their way into the center of his life and had shown him just how barren it had been.

But when they left, his life would slide back onto its original course and the silence would seem even deeper. And God, he didn't like the thought of that.

Sam frowned. "Why are we really here?"

"To eat that amazing steak, for one," Joy said, sipping at her wine. Interesting, she thought, how his facial expressions gave hints to what he was thinking. And even more interesting how fast a smile from him could dissolve into the more familiar scowl. She'd have given a lot in that moment to know exactly what was running through his mind.

"And for another?"

"To show you how nice the people of Franklin are. To prove to you that you can meet people without turning into a pillar of salt..." She sat back, sipped at her wine again and kept her voice lighter than she felt. "Admit it. You had a good time."

"The steak was good," he said grudgingly, but she saw a flash of a smile that appeared and disappeared in a heartbeat.

"And the company."

His gaze fixed on hers. "You already know I like the company."

"I do," she said and felt a swirl of nerves flutter into life in the pit of her belly. Why was it this man who could make her feel things she'd never felt before? Life would have been so much easier if she'd found some nice, uncomplicated guy to fall for. But then she wouldn't be able to look into those golden-brown eyes of his, would she? "But you had a good time talking to other people, too. It just makes you uncomfortable hearing compliments."

"Think you know me, don't you?"

"Yep," she said, smiling at him in spite of the spark of irritation in his eyes. Just as Holly had once said, *he's not mean, he's just crabby.* He didn't fool her anymore. Even when he was angry, it didn't last. Even when she ambushed him with knowledge of his past, he didn't cling to the fury that had erupted inside him. Even when he didn't want to spend time with a child, he went out of his way to make her dreams come true.

Joy's heart ached with all she was feeling, and she wondered if he could see it in her eyes.

The room was crowded. The log walls were smoke-stained from years of exposure to the wood fireplace that even now boasted a roaring blaze. People sat at round tables and a few leather booths along one wall while the wall facing Main Street was floor-to-ceiling windows, displaying the winter scene unfolding outside. Tonight, the music pumping through the speakers overhead was classical, something weepy with strings and piano. And sitting across the table from her, looking like he'd rather be anywhere else but there, was the man who held her heart.

Stupid? Maybe. But there was no going back for Joy now. She'd been stumbling over him a little every day, of course. His kindness to Holly. His company in the dead of night when the house sat quiet around them. His kiss. The way his eyes flared with heat and more whenever he looked at her. His reluctant participation in the "family" dinners in the dining room. All of those things had been drawing her in, making her fall.

But today, she'd simply taken the final plunge.

He must have gone into town on his own and bought those silly little fairy lights. Then he'd sneaked out into the freezing cold late at night when he wouldn't be seen. And he'd decorated those tiny houses because her little girl had believed. He'd given Holly that. Magic.

Sam had sparked her imagination, protected her dreams and her fantasies. Joy had watched her baby girl throw herself into the arms of the man she trusted, loved, and through a sheen of tears had seen Sam hold Holly as tenderly as if she'd been made of glass. And in that one incredible moment, Joy told herself, he'd completely won her heart. Whether he wanted it or not was a different question.

She, Joy thought, was toast.

He could pretend to be aloof, crabby, disinterested all he wanted now, and she wouldn't believe it. He'd given her daughter a gift beyond price and she would always love him for that.

"What?" he asked, frowning a little harder. "What is it?"

She shook her head. "Nothing."

The frown came back instantly. "Makes a man nervous when a woman gets that thoughtful look in her eyes."

"Nervous is good, though I doubt," she said quietly, "that you ever have to worry about nerves."

"You might be surprised," he murmured, then said more firmly, "Let's go before the storm settles in and we're stuck down here."

Right then, Joy couldn't think of anywhere she'd rather be than back in that amazing house, alone with Sam. She looked him dead in the eye and said softly, "Good idea."

The ride up the mountain seemed to take forever, or maybe it was simply because Joy felt so on edge it was as if her skin was one size too tight. Every inch of her buzzed with anticipation because she knew what she wanted and knew she was done waiting. The tension between them had been building for days now, and tonight, she wanted to finally release it. To revel in being with a man she loved—even if she couldn't tell him how she felt.

At the house, they left the car in the garage and walked through the connecting door into the mudroom, where they hung their jackets on hooks before heading into the kitchen. Joy hit a switch on the wall, and the soft lights above the table blinked into life. Most of the room was still dark, and that was just as she wanted it. When she turned to Sam, she went up on her toes, cupped his face in her palms and kissed him, putting everything she was feeling into it.

Her heartbeat jumped into a frantic rhythm, her stomach swirled with excitement and the ache that had been building inside her for days began to pulse. It took only a second for Sam to react. To have his arms come around her. He lifted her off her feet, and she wrapped herself around him like a ribbon around a present.

As if he'd only been awaiting her signal, he took her with a desperation that told Joy he wanted her as much as she wanted him. She *felt* the hunger pumping off him in thick waves and gave herself up to it, letting it feed her own until a raging storm overtook them both. His mouth covered hers, his tongue demanding entry. She gave way and sighed in growing need as he groaned and kissed her harder, deeper.

His hands, those talented, strong hands, dropped to her bottom. He turned her around so fast her stomach did a wild spin, then he slammed her up against the back door. Joy hardly felt it. She'd never experienced anything like what swept over her in those few frantic moments. Every inch of her body was alive with sensations. Her skin was buzzing, her blood boiling, and her mind was a tangled, hazy mass of thoughts that pretty much went, *yes, harder, now, be inside me.*

Her fingers scraped through his hair, held his head to hers. Every breath came strangled, harsh, and she didn't care. All she wanted, all she needed, was the taste of him filling her. The feel of his hands holding her. Then, when she became light-headed, she thought, okay, maybe air, too.

She broke the kiss, letting her head drop back as she gasped for breath. Staring up at the dimly lit ceiling, she concentrated solely on the feel of Sam's mouth at her throat, latching on to the pulse point at the base of her neck. He tasted, he nibbled, he licked, and she sighed heavily.

"Oh, boy. That feels really…" She gasped again. *"Good."*

With his mouth against her throat, he smiled. "You taste good, too."

"Thanks." She chuckled and the sound bubbled up into the room. "Always good to hear."

"I've wanted my hands on you for days." He lifted his head and waited for her to look at him. His eyes were alight with a fire that seemed to be sweeping both of them along in an inferno. "I tried to keep my distance, but it's been killing me."

"Me, too," she said, holding him a little tighter. "I've been dreaming about you."

One corner of his mouth lifted. "Yeah? Well, time to wake up." He let her slide down the length of his body until she was on her feet again. "Let's go."

"Where?"

"Upstairs, where the beds are." He started pulling her. "After waiting this long, we're not doing this on the kitchen floor."

Right about then, Joy thought, the floor looked pretty good. Or the granite island. Or just the stupid wall she'd been up against a second ago. Especially since her knees felt like rubber and she wasn't sure she'd make it all the way up those stairs. Then she realized they didn't have to.

"Yeah, but my bed's quicker." She gave a tug, too, then grinned when he looked at her in admiration.

"Good thinking. I do like a smart woman." He scooped her up again, this time cradling her in his arms, and headed for Kaye's suite.

"Well, I always wanted to be swept off my feet." Really, her poor, foolish heart was stuttering at being carried off to bed. The romance of it tugged at everything inside her. He stepped into the darkened suite, and she hit the light switch for the living area as he passed it.

Instantly, the tiny, misshapen Christmas tree

burst into electric life. Softly glowing lights burned steadily all around the room, but it was the silly tree that had center stage.

"What the—" He stopped, his grip on her tightening, and let his gaze sweep around the room. So Joy looked, too, admiring all she and Holly had done to their temporary home. Sam hadn't wanted the holidays leaking out into the main house, so they'd gone overboard here, in their corner of it. Christmas lights lined the doorways and were draped across the walls like garland. The tiny tree stood on a table and was practically bowed under the weight of the ornaments, popped corn and strings of lights adorning it.

After a long minute or two, he shook his head. "That tree is sad."

"It is not," she argued, spearing it with a critical eye. "It's loved." She looked past the tree in the window to the night outside and the fairy lights just visible through the swirls of snow, and her heart dissolved all over again. Cupping his cheek in her palm, she turned his face to hers. "You lit up Holly's world today with those strings of lights."

He scowled but there wasn't much punch to it. "I hated seeing her check for signs every day and not getting any. But she never stopped believing."

Her heart actually filled up and spilled over into her chest. How could she *not* love a man who'd given life to her baby's imagination?

"I put 'em on a timer," Sam said, "so they'll go off

and on at different times and Holly will have something to watch for."

Shaking her head, she looked into his eyes and whispered, "I don't have the words for what I'm feeling right now."

"Then we're lucky. No words required."

He kissed her again and Joy surrendered to the fire. She forgot about everything else but the taste of him, the feel of him. She wanted to stroke her hands all over his leanly muscled body, feel the warm slide of flesh to flesh. Lifting her face, she nibbled at his throat and smiled when she heard him groan tightly.

She hardly noticed when he carried her through the main room and dropped her onto her bed. *Wild*, was all she could think. Wild for him, for his touch, for his taste. She'd been alone for so long, having this man, *the* man with her, was almost more than she could stand.

He felt the same, because in a few short seconds, they were both naked, clothes flying around the room as they tore at them until there was nothing separating them. The quilt on the bed felt cool beneath her, but he was there, sliding on top of her, to bring the heat.

"Been wanting to peel you out of those sweaters you wear for days now," he murmured, trailing kisses up from her belly to just below her breasts.

"Been wanting you to do it," she assured him and ran the flat of her hands over his shoulders in long, sensuous strokes.

His hands moved over her, following every line, every curve. She gasped when he dipped his head to take first one hard nipple then the other into his mouth. Damp heat fractured something inside her as his teeth, tongue, lips teased at her sensitive skin. She was writhing mindlessly, chasing the need, when he dipped one hand to her center and cupped her heat completely.

Joy's mind simply splintered from the myriad sensations slamming into her system all at once. She hadn't felt this way in…ever. He shifted, kissing her mouth, tangling his tongue with hers as those oh-so-talented fingers dipped inside her heat. She lifted her hips into his touch and held his head to hers as they kissed, as they took and gave and then did it all again. Their breath mingled, their hearts pounded in a wild tandem that raced faster and faster as they tasted, explored, discovered.

It was like being caught in a hurricane. There was no safe place to hide, even if she'd wanted to. And she didn't. She wanted the storm, more than she'd ever wanted anything in her life. Demand, need, hands reaching, mouths seeking. Hushed words flew back and forth between them, whispers, breathless sighs. Heat ratcheted up in the tiny bedroom as outside, the snow fell, draping the world in icy white.

Sam's hand at her core drove her higher, faster. A small ripple of release caught her and had Joy calling his name as she shivered, shuddered in response.

But she'd barely recovered from that tiny explosion before he pushed her again. His fingers danced over her body, inside and out, caressing, stroking until she thought she'd lose what was left of her mind if he didn't get inside her. Now.

Whimpering, Joy didn't care. All she could think of was the release she wanted more than her next breath. "Be inside me," she told him, voice breaking on every word as air struggled in and out of her lungs.

"Now," he agreed in a strained whisper.

Shadows filled the room, light from the snow, reflections of the lights in the living area. He took her mouth again in a frenzied kiss that stole her breath and gave her his. She arched into him as he moved over her, parting her thighs and sliding into her with one long thrust.

Joy gasped, her head tipping back into the pillow, her hips lifting to welcome him, to take him deeper. His hands held her hips, his fingers digging into her skin as he drove into her again and again. She locked her legs around his hips, pulling him tighter to her, rocking with him, following the frenzied rhythm he set.

The storm claimed them. Hunger roared up into the room and overtook them both. There was nothing in the world but that need and the race to completion. Their bodies moved together, skin to skin, breath to breath. They raced to the edge of the cliff together, and together they took the leap, locked in each other's arms.

"I think I'm blind."

Sam pushed off her and rolled to one side. "Open your eyes."

"Oh. Right." She looked at him and Sam felt the solid punch of her gaze slam into him. His body was still humming, his blood still pounding in his ears. He'd just had the most intense experience of his life and he wanted her again. Now.

He stroked one hand down her body, following the curve of breast to belly to hip. She shivered and he smiled. He couldn't touch her enough. The feel of her was addictive. How could his craving for her be as sharp now as it had been before? He should be relaxed. Instead, he felt more fired up. The need building inside him was sharper now because he *knew* what he'd been missing. Knew what it was to be inside her, to feel her wrapped around him, holding him tight. To look into her eyes and watch passion burst like fireworks on the Fourth.

It felt as if cold, iron bands were tightening around his chest. Danger. He knew it. He knew that feeling anything for Joy was a one-way trip to disaster, pain and misery. Yet it seemed that he didn't have any choice about that.

"Well." She blew out a breath and gave him a smile that had his body going rock hard again. "That was amazing. But I'm suddenly so thirsty I could drink a gallon of water."

"I'll get some," he told her, "as soon as I'm sure my legs will hold me."

"Isn't that a nice thing to say? There's no hurry," she said, turning into him, snuggling close. She buried her face in the curve of his neck and gave a sigh. "Here's good."

"Here's great." He rolled onto his back, pulling her over with him until she lay sprawled across his chest. Her blond curls tumbled around her face and her eyes sparkled in the dim light. "You caught me by surprise with that kiss."

She folded her arms on his chest and grinned down at him. "Well, then, you have an excellent reaction time."

"Not complaining." He hadn't been prepared for that kiss, and it had pushed him right over the edge of the control he'd been clinging to for days. Wincing a little, he thought he should have taken his time with her. To slowly drive them both to the breaking point. Instead, he'd been hit by an unstoppable force and hadn't been able to withstand it. They'd rushed together so quickly he hadn't—Sam went completely still as reality came crashing down on him, obliterating the buzz of satisfaction as if it had never been.

"What is it? Sam?"

He looked up into her eyes and called himself every kind of name he could think of. How could he have been so stupid? So careless? It was too late now, he told himself grimly. Too late to do anything but worry. "Joy, the downside to things happening by surprise is you're not prepared for it."

She smiled. "I'd say you were plenty prepared."

He rolled again, flopping her over onto the mattress and leaning over her, staring her in the eyes. "I'm trying to tell you that I hope to hell you're on birth control because I wasn't suited up."

Nine

Sam watched her as, for a second or two, she just stared at him as if she were trying to make sense of a foreign language. And since he was staring into those clear blue eyes of hers, he *saw* the shift of emotions when what he'd said finally sunk in.

And even then, the uppermost thought in his mind was her scent and how it clung to her skin and seeped into his bones. Every breath he drew pulled her inside him, until summer flowers filled every corner of his heart, his soul.

What the hell was wrong with him? *Focus.* He'd led them both into a risky situation, and he had to keep his mind on what could, potentially, be facing them. It had been a long time since he'd been with anyone, sure. But it was Joy herself who had blown all thought, all reason, right out of his head with that one surprise kiss in the kitchen. After that, all he'd been able to think about was getting her naked. To finally have her under him, over him. He'd lost control for the first time in his life, and even though the consequences could be steep, he couldn't really regret any of it.

"Oh. Well." Joy lifted one hand and pushed his hair back from his face. Her touch sent a fresh new jolt of need blasting through him, and he had to grit his teeth in the effort to hold on to what was left of the tattered threads of his control.

"Are you," he asked, voice tight, "on birth control?"

"No."

One word. One simple word that hit the pit of his stomach like a ball of ice. "Okay. Look. This is my fault, Joy. I shouldn't have…"

"Fault? If you're looking to place blame here, you're on your own," she said, sliding her fingers through his hair. "This isn't on you alone, so don't look like you're about to be blindfolded and stood up against a wall in front of a firing squad."

He frowned and wondered when he'd become so easy to read.

"You weren't alone in this room, Sam," she said. "This is on me as much as you. We got…carried away—"

He snorted. "Yeah, you could say that."

"—and we didn't think. We weren't prepared," she finished as if he hadn't interrupted her.

He laughed shortly but there was no humor behind it. This had to be the damnedest after-sex conversation he'd ever had. He should have known that Joy wouldn't react as he would have expected her to. No recriminations, no gnashing of teeth, just simple acceptance for what couldn't be changed.

Still. "That's the thing," he said with a shake of his head. "I thought I was. Prepared, I mean. When I went into town to get those damn fairy lights, I also bought condoms."

She drew her head back and grinned down at him. "You're kidding. Really?"

"Yes, really. They're upstairs. In my room."

She laughed and shook her head. "That's perfect. Well, in your defense, you did try to get me upstairs…"

"True." But they probably wouldn't have made it, as hot as they'd both been. Most likely, they'd have stopped and had at each other right there on the stairs anyway.

"And I love that you bought condoms," she said, planting a soft kiss on his mouth. "I love that you wanted me as much as I wanted you."

"No question about that," he admitted, though the rest of this situation was settling in like rain clouds over an outdoor party.

"But you realize that now everyone in Franklin knows you bought them."

"What?"

"Oh, yes," she said, nodding sagely. "By now, word has spread all over town and everyone is speculating about just what's going on up here."

"Perfect." Small-town life, he told himself, knowing she was right. He hadn't thought about it. Hadn't considered that by buying condoms at the local pharmacy he was also feeding fuel to the gossip. It had been so long since he'd been part of a community that he hadn't given it a thought, but now he remembered the speculative gleam in the cashier's eye. The smile on the face of the customer behind him in line. "Damn."

"We're the talk of the town," Joy assured him, still smiling. "I've always wanted to be gossiped about."

All of that aside for the moment, Sam couldn't understand how she could be so damned amused by any of this. All he could feel was the bright flash of panic hovering on the edges of his mind. By being careless, he might have created a child. He'd lost a child already. Lost his son. How could he make another and not have his heart ripped out of his chest?

"Forget what people are saying, Joy," he said, and his tone, if nothing else, erased her smile. "Look, whatever happens—"

"You can get that unnerved look off your face," she said softly. "I'm a big girl, Sam. I can take care of myself. You don't owe me anything, and I don't need you to worry about me or what might happen."

"I'll decide what I owe, Joy," he told her. It didn't matter what she said, Sam told himself. He would worry anyway. He laid one hand on her belly and let it lay there, imagining what might already be happening deep within her.

"Sam." She cupped his face in her hands and waited until he looked into her eyes. "Stop thinking. Can we just enjoy what we shared? Leave it at that?"

His heartbeat thundered in his chest. Just her touch was enough to push him into forgetting everything but her. Everything but this moment. He wanted her even more than he had before and didn't know how that was possible. She was staring up at him with those wide blue eyes of hers, and Sam thought he could lose himself in those depths. Maybe she was right. At least for now, for this moment, maybe it was better if they stopped thinking, worrying, wondering. Because these moments were all they had. All they would ever have.

He wasn't going to risk loss again. He wouldn't put his soul up as a hostage to fate, by falling in love, having another family that the gods could snatch from him. A future for them was out of the question. But they had tonight, didn't they?

"Come with me," he said, rolling off the bed and taking her hand to pull her up with him.

"What? Why? Where?"

"My room. Where the condoms live." He kept pulling her after him and she half ran to keep up. "We can stop and get water—or wine—on the way up."

"Wine. Condoms." She tugged him to a stop, then plastered herself against him until he felt every single inch of her body pressed along his. Then she stepped back. "Now, that kind of thinking is a good thing. I like your plan. Just let me get my robe."

Amazing woman. She could be wild and uninhibited in bed but quailed about walking naked through an empty house.

"You don't need a robe. We're the only ones here. There are no neighbors for five miles in any direction, so no one can look in the windows."

"It's cold so I still want it," she said, lifting one hand to cup his cheek.

For a second, everything stopped for Sam. He just stared at her. In the soft light, her skin looked like fine porcelain. Her hair was a tumbled mass of gold and her eyes were as clear and blue as the lake. Her seductively sly smile curved a mouth that was made to be kissed. If he were still an artist, Sam thought, he'd want to paint her like this. Just as she was now.

That knowing half smile on her face, one arm lifted toward him, with the soft glow of Christmas lights behind her. She looked, he thought, like a pagan goddess, a woman born to be touched, adored, and that's how he would paint her. If he still painted, which he didn't. And why didn't he?

Because he'd lost the woman he'd once loved. A woman who had looked at him as Joy did now. A woman who had given him a son and then taken him with her when she left.

Pain grabbed his heart and squeezed.

Instantly, she reacted. "Sam? What is it?"

"I want you," he said, moving in on her, backing her into the wall, looking down into her eyes.

"I know, I feel the same way."

He nodded, swallowed hard, then forced the words out because they had to be said. Even if she pulled away from him right now, they had to be said. "But if you're thinking there's a future here for us, don't. I'm not that guy. Not anymore."

"Sam—" Her hands slid up and down his arms, and he was grateful for the heat she kindled inside him. "I didn't ask you for anything."

"I don't want to hurt you, Joy." Yet he knew he would. She was the kind of woman who would spin dreams for herself, her daughter. She would think about futures. As a mother, she had to. As a former father, he couldn't. Not again. Just the thought of it sharpened the pain in his heart. If he was smart, he'd end this with Joy right now.

But apparently, he had no sense at all.

She gave him another smile and went up on her toes to kiss him gently. "I told you. You don't have to worry about me, Sam. I know what I'm doing."

He wished that were true. But there would be time

enough later for regrets, for second-guessing decisions made in the night. For now, there was Joy.

A few days later, Joy was upstairs, looking out Sam's bedroom window at the workshop below. Holly was out there with Sam right now, probably working on more fairy houses. Since the first two were now filled with fairy families, Holly was determined to put up a housing development at the foot of the woods.

Her smile was wistful as she turned away and looked at the big bed with the forest green comforter and mountain of pillows. She hadn't been with Sam up here since that first night. He came to her now, in Kaye's room, where they made love with quiet sighs and soft whispers so they wouldn't wake Holly in the next room. And after hours wrapped together, Sam left her bed early in the morning so the little girl wouldn't guess what was happening.

It felt secret and sad and wonderful all at the same time. Joy was in love and couldn't tell him because she knew he didn't want to hear it. She might be pregnant and knew he wouldn't want to hear that, either. Every morning when he left her, she felt him go just a bit further away. And one day soon, she knew, he wouldn't come back. He was distancing himself from her, holding back emotionally so that when she left at the end of the month he wouldn't miss her.

Why couldn't he see that he didn't *have* to miss

her? It was almost impossible to believe she'd known Sam for less than three weeks. He was so embedded in her heart, in her life, she felt as if she'd known him forever. As if they'd been meant to meet, to find each other. To be together. If only Sam could see that as clearly as Joy did.

The house phone rang and she answered without looking at the caller ID. "Henry residence."

"Joy? Oh, it's so nice to finally talk to you!" A female voice, happy.

"Thanks," she said, carrying the phone back to the window so she could look outside. "Who is this?"

"God, how stupid of me," the woman said with a delighted laugh. "I'm Catherine Henry, Sam's mother."

Whoa. A wave of embarrassment swept over her. Joy was standing in Sam's bedroom, beside the bed where they'd had sex, and talking to his mother. Could this be any more awkward? "Hello. Um, Sam's out in the workshop."

"Oh, I know," she said and Joy could almost see her waving one hand to dismiss that information. "I just talked to him and your adorable daughter, Holly."

"You did?" Confused, she stared down at the workshop and watched as Sam and Holly walked out through the snow covering the ground. Sam was carrying the latest fairy house and Holly, no surprise, was chattering a mile a minute. Joy's heart ached with pleasure and sorrow.

"Holly tells me that she and Sam are making houses for fairies and that my son isn't as crabby as he used to be."

"Oh, for—" Joy closed her eyes briefly. "I'm so sorry—"

"Don't be silly. He *is* crabby," Catherine told her. "But he certainly seemed less so around your little girl."

"He's wonderful with her."

There was a pause and then a sniffle as if the woman was fighting tears. "I'm so glad. I've hoped for a long time to see my son wake up again. Find happiness again. It sounds to me like he is."

"Oh," Joy spoke up quickly, shaking her head as if Sam's mother could see her denial, "Mrs. Henry—"

"Catherine."

"Fine. Catherine, please don't make more of this than there is. Sam doesn't want—"

"Maybe not," she interrupted. "But he needs. So much. He's a good man, Joy. He's just been lost."

"I know," Joy answered on a sigh, resting her hand on the ice-cold windowpane as she watched the man she loved and her daughter kneeling together in the snow. "But what if he doesn't want to be found?"

Another long pause and Catherine said, "Kaye's told me so much about you, Joy. She thinks very highly of you, and just speaking to your daughter tells me that you're a wonderful mother."

"I hope so," she said, her gaze fixed on Sam.

"Look, I don't know how you feel, but if you don't mind my saying, I can hear a lot in your voice when you speak of Sam."

"Catherine—" If she couldn't tell Sam how she felt she certainly couldn't tell his *mother*.

"You don't have to say anything, dear. Just please. Do me a favor and don't give up on him."

"I don't want to." Joy could admit that much. "I… care about him."

"I'm so glad." The next pause was a short one. "After the holidays I'm going to come and visit Sam. I hope we can meet then."

"I'd like that," Joy said and meant it. She just hoped that she would still be seeing Sam by then.

When the phone call ended a moment later, she hung up the phone and walked back to the window to watch the two people in the world she loved most.

"Will more fairies move in and put up some more lights like the other ones did?" Holly asked, kneeling in the snow to peek through the windows of the tiny houses.

"We'll have to wait and see, I guess," Sam told her, setting the new house down on a flat rock slightly above the others.

"I bet they do because now they have friends here and—"

Sam smiled to himself as the little girl took off on another long, rambling monologue. He was going to miss spending time with Holly. As much as he'd fought against it in the beginning, the little girl had wormed her way into his heart—just like her mother had. In his own defense, Sam figured there weren't many people who could have ignored a five-year-old with as much charm as this one. Even the cold didn't diminish her energy level. If anything, he thought, it pumped her up. Her little cheeks were rosy, her eyes, so much like her mother's, sparkled.

"Do fairies have Christmas trees?"

"What?"

"Like Mommy and me got a tiny little tree because you don't like Christmas, but maybe if you had a great big tree you'd like Christmas more, Sam."

He slid a glance at her. He'd caught on to Holly's maneuvers. She was giving him that sly smile that he guessed females were born knowing how to deliver.

"You want a big Christmas tree," he said.

"I like our little one, but I like big ones, too, and we could make it really pretty with candy canes and we could make popcorn and put it on, too, and I think you'd like it."

"I probably would," he admitted. Hell, just because he was against Christmas didn't mean a five-year-old had to put up with a sad little tree tucked away in her room. "Why don't you go get your mom and we'll cut down a tree."

Her eyes went wide. "Cut it down ourselves? In the woods?"

"You bet. You can help." As long as he had his hands over hers on the hatchet, showing her how to do it without risking her safety. Around them, the pines rustled in the wind and sounded like sighs. The sky was heavy and gray and looked ready to spill another foot or two of snow any minute. "You can pick out the tree—as long as it's not a giant," he added with a smile.

She studied him thoughtfully for so long, he had to wonder what she was thinking. Nothing could have prepared him, though, for what she finally said. "You're a good daddy."

He sat back on his heels to look at her, stunned into silence. Snow was seeping into the legs of his jeans, but he paid no attention. "What?"

"You're a good daddy," she said again and moved up to lay one hand on his cheek. "You help me with stuff and you show me things and I know you used to have a little boy but he had to go to heaven with his mommy and that's what makes you crabby."

Air caught in his chest. Couldn't exhale or inhale. All he could do was watch the child watching him.

How did she know about Eli? Had her mother told her? Or had she simply overheard other adults talking about him? Kids, he knew, picked up on more than the grown-ups around them ever noticed. As Holly watched him, she looked so serious. So solemn, his heart broke a little.

"But if you want," she went on, her perpetually

high-pitched, fast-paced voice softening, "I could be your little girl and you could be *my* daddy and then you wouldn't be crabby or lonely anymore."

His heart stopped. He felt it take one hard beat and then clutch. Her eyes were filled with a mixture of sadness and hope, and that steady gaze scorched him. This little girl was offering all the love a five-year-old held and hoping he'd take it. But how could he? How could he love a child again and risk losing that child? But wasn't he going to lose her anyway? Because of his own fears and the nightmares that had never really left him?

Sam had been so careful, for years, to stay isolated, to protect his heart, to keep his distance from the world at large. And now there was a tiny girl who had pierced through his defenses, showing him just how vulnerable he really was.

She was still looking at him, still waiting, trusting that he would want her. Love her.

He did. He already loved her, and that wasn't something he could admit. Not to himself. Not to the child who needed him. Sam had never thought of himself as a coward, but damned if he didn't feel like one now. How could he give her what she needed when the very thought of loving and losing could bring him to his knees?

He stood up, grabbed her and pulled her in for a tight hug, and her little arms went around his neck and clung as if her life depended on it. There at the edge of the woods with fairy magic shining in the gray, he was humbled by a little girl, shattered by the love freely offered.

"Do you want to be my daddy, Sam?" she whispered.

How to get out of this without hurting her? Without ripping his own heart out of his chest? Setting her down again, he crouched in front of her and met those serious blue eyes. "I'm proud you would ask me, Holly," he said, knowing just how special that request had been. "But this is pretty important, so I think you should talk to your mom about this first, okay?"

Not a no, not a yes. He didn't want to hurt her, but he couldn't give her what she wanted, either. Joy knew her daughter best. She would know how to let her down without crushing that very tender heart. And Joy knew—because he'd told her—that there was no future for them. What surprised him, though, was how much he wished things were different— that he could have told that little girl he would be her daddy and take care of her and love her. But he couldn't do it. Wouldn't do it.

"Okay, Sam." Holly grinned and her eyes lit up. "I'll go ask her right now, okay? And then we can show her the new fairy house and then we can get our big tree and maybe have hot chocolate and—" She took off at a dead run, still talking, still planning.

He turned to look at the house and saw Joy in the bedroom window, watching them. Would he always see her there, he wondered? Would he walk through his empty house and catch the faint scent of summer flowers? Would he sit in the great room at night and wait for her to come in and sit beside him? Smile at him? Would he spend the rest of his life reaching across the bed for her?

A few weeks ago, his life was insular, quiet, filled with the shadows of memories and the ghosts he carried with him everywhere. Now there would be *more* ghosts. The only difference being, he would have *chosen* to lose Joy and Holly.

That thought settled in, and he didn't like it. Still looking up at Joy, Sam asked himself if maybe he was wrong to pass up this opportunity. Maybe it was time to step out of the shadows. To take a chance. To risk it all.

A scream ripped his thoughts apart and in an instant, everything changed. Again.

Five stitches, three hot chocolates and one Christmas tree later, they were in the great room, watching the lights on the big pine in the front window shine. They'd used the strings of lights Joy had hung on the walls in their room, and now the beautiful pine was dazzling. There were popcorn chains and candy canes they'd bought in town as decorations. And there was an exhausted but happy little girl, asleep on the couch, a smile still curving her lips.

Joy brushed Holly's hair back from her forehead

and kissed the neat row of stitches. It had been a har-
rowing, scary ride down the mountain to the clinic
in town. But Sam had been a rock. Steady, confi-
dent, he'd already had Holly in his arms heading for
his truck by the time Joy had come downstairs at a
dead run.

Hearing her baby scream, watching her fall and
then seeing the bright splotch of blood on the snow
had shaken Joy right down to the bone. But Holly
was crying and reaching for her, so she swallowed
her own fear to try to ease Holly's. The girl had hit
her head on a rock under the snow when she fell. A
freak accident, but seeing the neat row of stitches
reminded Joy how fragile her child was. How easily
hurt. Physically. Emotionally.

Sam stood by the tree. "You want me to carry her
to bed?"

"Sure. Thanks."

He nodded and stalked across the room as if
every step was vibrating with repressed energy. But
when he scooped Holly into his arms, he was gen-
tle. Careful. She followed after him and neither of
them spoke again until Holly was tucked in with her
favorite stuffed dog and they were safely out in the
great room again.

Sam walked to the fireplace, stared down into
the flames as if looking for answers to questions he
hadn't asked, and shoved both hands into his pockets.
Joy walked over to join him, hooked her arm through

his and wasn't really surprised when he moved away. Hurt, yes. But not surprised.

She'd known this was coming. Maybe Holly being hurt had sped up the process, but Joy had been expecting him to pull away. To push her aside. He had been honest from the beginning, telling her that they had no future. That he didn't want forever because, she knew, he didn't trust in promises.

He cared for her. He cared for Holly, but she knew he didn't want to and wouldn't want to hear how much she loved him, so she kept it to herself. Private pain she could live with. She didn't think she could bear him throwing her love back in her face and dismissing it.

"Sam…"

"Scared me," he admitted in a voice so low she almost missed the words beneath the hiss and snap of the fire.

"I know," Joy said softly. "Me, too. But Holly's fine, Sam. The doctor said she wouldn't even have a scar."

"Yeah, and I'm glad of that." He shook his head and looked at her, firelight and shadow dancing over his features, glittering in his eyes. "But I can't do this again, Joy."

"Do what?" Heart aching, she took a step toward him, then stopped when he took one back.

"You know damn well what," he ground out. Then he took a deep breath and blew it out. "The thing is, just before Holly got hurt, I was thinking that maybe

I could. Maybe it was time to try again." He looked at her. "With you."

Hope rose inside her and then crashed again when he continued.

"Then that little girl screamed, and I knew I was kidding myself." Shaking his head slowly, he took another deep breath. "I lost my family once, Joy. I won't risk that kind of pain again. You and Holly have to go."

"If we go," she reminded him, "you *still* lose us."

He just stared at her. He didn't have an answer to that, and they both knew it.

"Yeah, I know. But you'll be safe out there and I won't have to wonder and worry every time you leave the damn house."

"So you'll never think of us," she mused aloud. "Never wonder what we're doing, if we're safe, if we're happy."

"I didn't say that," he pointed out. "But I can block that out."

"Yeah, you're good at blocking out."

"It's a gift." The smile that touched his mouth was wry, unhappy and gone in an instant.

"So just like that?" she asked, her voice low, throbbing with banked emotions that were nearly choking her. "We leave and what? You go back to being alone in this spectacular cage?" She lifted both hands to encompass the lovely room and said, "Because no matter how beautiful it is, it's still a *cage*, Sam."

"And it's my business." His voice was clipped, cold, as if he'd already detached from the situation. From *her*.

Well, she wasn't going to make it that easy on him.

"It's not just your business, Sam. It's mine. It's Holly's. She told me she asked you to be her daddy. Did that mean nothing to you?"

"It meant *everything*," he said, his voice a growl of pain and anger. "It's not easy to turn away from you. From her."

"Then don't do it."

"I have to."

Fury churned in the pit of her stomach and slid together with a layer of misery that made Joy feel sick to her soul. "How could I be in love with a man so stubborn he refuses to see what's right in front of him?"

He jolted. "Who said anything about love?"

"I did," she snapped. She wasn't going to walk away from him never saying how she felt. If he was going to throw her away like Mike had, like every foster parent she'd ever known had, then he would do it knowing the full truth. "I love you."

"Well," he advised, "*stop*."

She choked out a laugh that actually scraped at her throat. Amazing. As hurt as she was, she could still be amused by the idiot man who was willing to toss aside what most people never found. "Great. Good idea. I'll get right on that."

He grabbed her upper arms and drew her up until they were eye to eye. "Damn it, Joy, I told you up front that I'm not that guy. That there was no future for us."

"Yes, I guess I'm a lousy listener." She pulled away from him, cleared her throat and blinked back a sheen of tears because she *refused* to cry in front of him. "It must be your immense load of charm that dragged me in. That warm, welcoming smile."

He scowled at her.

"No, it was the way that you grudgingly bent to having us here. It was your gentleness with Holly, your sense of humor, your kiss, your touch, the way you look at me sometimes as if you don't know quite what to do with me." She smiled sadly. "I fell in love and there's no way out for me now. You're it, Sam."

He scrubbed one hand across his face as if he could wipe away her words, her feelings.

"You don't have to love me, Sam." That about killed her to say, but it was truth.

"I didn't want to hurt you, Joy."

"I believe you. But when you *care*, you hurt. That's life. But if you don't love me, try to love someone else." Oh God, the thought of that tore what was left of her heart into tiny, confetti-sized pieces. "But stop hiding out here in this palace of shadows and live your life."

"I like my life."

"No you don't," she countered, voice thick with

those unshed tears. "Because you don't have one. What you have is sacrifice."

He pushed both hands through his hair then let them fall to his sides. "What the hell are you talking about?"

She took a breath, steadying herself, lowering her voice, *willing* him to hear her. "You've locked yourself away, Sam. All to punish yourself for surviving. What happened to your family was terrible, I can't even imagine the pain you lived through. But you're still alive, Sam. Staying closed down and shut off won't alter what happened. It won't bring them back."

His features went tight, cold, his eyes shuttered as they had been so often when she first met him.

"You think I don't know that?" He paced off a few steps, then whirled around and came right back. His eyes glittered with banked fury and pain. "Nothing will bring them back. Nothing can change why they died, either."

"What?" Confused, worried, she waited.

"You know why I had to drive you into town for Holly's sleepover?"

"Of course I do." She shook her head, frowning. "My car wouldn't start."

"Because I took the damn distributor cap off."

That made no sense at all. "What? Why?"

Now he scrubbed his hands over his face and gave

a bitter sigh. "Because, I couldn't let you drive down the mountain in the snow."

"Sam…"

Firelight danced around the room but looked haunting as it shadowed his face, highlighting the grief carved into his features, like a mask in stone. As she watched him, she saw his eyes blur, focus on images in his mind rather than the woman who stood just opposite him.

"I was caught up in a painting," he said. "It was a commission. A big one and I wanted to keep at it while I was on a roll." He turned from her, set both hands on the fireplace mantel and stared down into the crackling flames. "There was a family reunion that weekend and Dani was furious that I didn't want to go. So I told her to take Eli and go ahead. That I'd meet her at the reunion as soon as I was finished." He swiveled his head to look at Joy. "She was on the interstate and a front tire blew. Dani lost control of the car and slammed into an oncoming semi. Both she and Eli died instantly."

Joy's heart ripped open, and the pain she felt for him nearly brought her to her knees. But she kept quiet, wanting him to finish and knowing he needed to get it all said.

"If I'd been driving it might have been different, but I'll never know, will I?" He pushed away from the mantel and glared at her, daring her to argue with him. "I chose my work over my family and I lost them. You once asked me why I don't paint anymore, and there's your reason. I chose my work over what should have been more important. So I don't paint. I don't go out. I don't—"

"Live," she finished for him. "You don't *live*, Sam. Do you really think that's what Dani would want for you? To spend the next fifty years locked away from everything and everyone? Is that how she wanted to live?"

"Of course not," he snapped.

"Then what's the point of the self-flagellation?" Joy demanded, walking toward him, ignoring the instinctive step back he took. "If you'd been in that car, you might have died, too."

"You don't know that."

"You don't, either. That's the point."

Outside, the wind moaned as it slid beneath the eaves. But tonight, it sounded louder, like a desperate keening, as if even the house was weeping for what was ending.

Trying again, Joy said, "My little girl loves you. I love you. Can you really let that go so easily?"

His gaze snapped to hers. "I told you that earlier today, I actually thought that maybe I could risk it. Maybe there was a chance. And then Holly was hurt and my heart stopped."

"Kids get hurt, Sam," she said, still trying, though she could see in his eyes that the fight was over. His decision was made whether she agreed or not. "We lose people we shouldn't. But life keeps going. *We* keep going. The world doesn't stop, Sam, and it shouldn't."

"Maybe not," he said softly. "But it's going to keep going without me."

Ten

Joy spent the next few days taking care of business. She buried the pain beneath layers of carefully constructed indifference and focused on what she had to do. In between taking care of her clients, she made meals for Sam and froze them. Whatever else happened after she left this house, he wouldn't starve.

If she had her way, she wouldn't leave. She'd stay right here and keep hammering at his hard head until she got through. And maybe, one day, she'd succeed. But then again, maybe not. So she couldn't take the chance. It was one thing to risk her own heart, but she wouldn't risk Holly's. Her daughter was already crazy about Sam. The longer they stayed here in this house, the deeper those feelings would go. And before long, Sam would break her baby's heart. He might not mean to, but it was inevitable.

Because he refused to love them back. Sooner or later, Holly would feel that and it would crush her. Joy wouldn't let that happen.

She would miss this place, though, she told herself as she packed up Holly's things. Glancing out the bedroom window, she watched her little girl and Sam placing yet another fairy house in the woods. And she had to give the man points for kindness.

She and Sam hadn't really spoken since that last night when everything had been laid out between them. They'd sidestepped each other when they could, and when they couldn't they'd both pretended that everything was fine. No point in upsetting Holly, after all. And despite—or maybe because of how strained things were between her and Sam—he hadn't changed toward Holly. That alone made her love him more and made it harder to leave. But tomorrow morning, she and Holly would wake up back in their own house in Franklin.

"Thank God Buddy finished the work early," she muttered, folding up the last of Holly's shirts and laying them in the suitcase.

Walking into the kitchen of her dreams, Joy sighed a little, then took out a pad of paper and a pen. Her heart felt heavy, the knot of emotion still stuck at the base of her throat, and every breath seemed like an event. She hated leaving. Hated walking away from

Sam. But she didn't have a choice any longer. Sitting on a stool at the granite counter, she made a list for Sam of the food she had stocked for him. There was enough food in the freezer now to see him through to when Kaye returned.

Would he miss her? she wondered. Would he sit in that dining room alone and remember being there with her and Holly? Would he sit in the great room at night and wish Joy was there beside him? Or would he wipe it all out of his mind? Would she become a story never talked about like his late wife? Was Joy now just another reason to block out life and build the barricades around his heart that much higher?

She'd hoped to pull Sam out of the shadows—now she might have had a hand in pushing him deeper into the darkness. Sighing a little, she got up, stirred the pot of beef stew, then checked the bread in the oven.

When she looked out the window again, she saw the fairy lights had blinked on and Holly was kneeling beside Sam in the snow. She couldn't hear what was being said, but her heart broke a little anyway when her daughter laid her little hand on Sam's shoulder. Leaving was going to be hard. Tearing Holly away was going to be a nightmare. But she had to do it. For everyone's sake.

Two hours later, Holly put on her stubborn face.

"But I don't wanna go," Holly shouted and pulled away from her mother to run down the hall to the great room. "Sam! Sam! Mommy says we're leaving and I don't want to go cuz we're building a fairy house and I have to help you put it in the woods so the fairies can come and—"

Joy walked into the main room behind her daughter and watched as Holly threw herself into Sam's lap. He looked at Joy over the child's head even as he gave the little girl a hug.

"Tell her we have to stay, Sam, cuz I'm your helper now and you need me."

"I do," he said, and his voice sounded rough, scratchy. "But your mom needs you, too, so if she says it's time to go, you're going to have to."

She tipped her head back, looking at him with rivers of tears in her eyes. "But I don't want to."

"I know. I don't want you to, either." He gave her what looked to Joy like a wistful smile, then tugged on one of her pigtails. "Why don't I finish up the fairy house and then bring it to you so you can give it to Lizzie."

She shook her head so hard, her pigtails whipped back and forth across her eyes. "It's not the same, Sam. Can't I stay?"

"Come on, Holly," Joy spoke up quickly because her own emotions were taking over. Tears were close, and watching her daughter's heart break was breaking her own. "We really have to go."

Holly threw her a furious look, brows locked down, eyes narrowed. "You're being mean."

"I'm your mom," Joy said tightly, keeping her own tears at bay. "That's my job. Now come on."

"I love you, Sam," Holly whispered loud enough for her voice to carry. Then she gave him a smacking kiss on the cheek and crawled off his lap. Chin on her chest, she walked toward Joy with slow, dragging steps, as if she was pulling each foot out of mud along the way.

Joy saw the stricken look on Sam's face and thought, *Good. Now you know what you've given up. What you're allowing yourself to lose.*

Head bowed, shoulders slumped, Holly couldn't have been more clear in her desolation. Well, Joy knew just how she felt. Taking the little girl's hand, she gave it a squeeze and said, "Let's go home, sweetie."

They headed out the front door, and Joy didn't look back. She couldn't. For the first time in days, the sun was out, and the only clouds in the sky were big and white and looked as soft and fluffy as Santa's beard. The pines were covered in snow, and the bare branches of the aspens and birches looked like they'd been decorated with lace as the snow lay on every tiny twig. It was magical. Beautiful.

And Joy took no pleasure in any of it.

Holly hopped into her car seat and buckled herself in while Joy did a quick check of everything stuffed into the car. Their tiny tree was in the backseat and their suitcases in the trunk. Holly sat there glowering at the world in general, and Joy sighed because she knew her darling daughter was going to make her life a living hell for the next few days at least.

"That's it then," Joy said, forcing a smile as she turned to look at Sam. He wore that black leather jacket, and his jeans were faded and stacked on the toes of his battered work boots. His hair was too long, his white long-sleeved shirt was open at the neck, and his brown eyes pinned her with an intensity that stole her breath.

"Drive safely."

"That's all you've got?" she asked, tipping her head to one side to study him.

"What is there left to say?" he countered. "Didn't we get it all said a few days ago?"

"Not nearly, but you still don't understand that, do you?" He stood on his drive with the well-lit splendor of his house behind him. In the front window, the Christmas tree they'd decorated together shone in a fiery blaze of color, and behind her, she knew, there were fairy lights shining at the edge of the woods.

She looked up at him, then moved in closer. He didn't move, just locked his gaze with hers as she approached. When she was close enough, she cupped his cheeks in her palms and said softly, "We would have been good for you, Sam. I would have been. You and I could have been happy together. We could have built something that most people only dream about." She went up on her toes, kissed his grim, unyielding mouth, then looked at him again. "I want you to remember something. When you lost your family there was nothing you could do about it. *This* time, it's your choice. You're losing and you're letting it happen."

His mouth tightened, his eyes flashed, but he didn't speak, and Joy knew it was over.

"I'm sorry for you," she said, "that you're allowing your own pain to swallow your life."

Before he could tell her to mind her own business, she turned and walked to the car. With Holly loudly complaining, she fired up the engine, put it in gear and drove away from Sam Henry and all the might-have-beens that would drive her crazy for the rest of her life.

For the next few days, Sam settled back into what his life was like pre-Joy and Holly. He worked on his secret project—that didn't really need to be a secret anymore, because he always finished what he started. He called his mother to check in because he should—but when she asked about Joy and Holly, he evaded, not wanting to talk about them any more than he wanted to think about them.

He tried to put the two females out of his mind, but how could he when he sensed Joy in every damn corner of his house?

In Kaye's suite, Joy's scent still lingered in the air. But the rooms were empty now. No toys, no stuffed dog. Joy's silky red robe wasn't hanging on the back of the door, and that pitiful excuse for a Christmas tree was gone as if it had never been there at all.

Every night, he sat in the great room in front of the fire and looked at the tree in the window. That it was there amazed him. Thinking about the night he and Joy and Holly had decorated it depressed him. For so many years, he'd avoided all mention of Christmas because he hadn't wanted to remember.

Now, though, he *did* want to. He relived every moment of the time Joy and Holly had been a part of his life. But mostly, he recalled the afternoon they had *left* him. He remembered Holly waving goodbye out the rear window of her mother's car. He remembered the look in Joy's eyes when she kissed him and told him that he was making a mistake by letting her go. And he particularly remembered Joy's laugh, her smile, the taste of her mouth and the feel of her arms around him when he was inside her.

Her image remained uppermost in his mind as if she'd been carved there. He couldn't shake it and didn't really want to. Remembering was all he had. The house was too damn quiet. Hell, he spent every day and most of the night out in the workshop just to avoid the suffocating silence. But it was no better out there because a part of him kept waiting for Holly to rush in, do one of her amazing monologues and climb up on the stool beside him.

When he was working, he found himself looking

at the house, half expecting to see Joy in one of the windows, smiling at him. And every time he didn't, another piece of him died. He'd thought that he could go back to his old life once they were gone. Slide back into the shadows, become again the man fate had made him. But that hadn't happened and now, he realized, it never could.

He wasn't the same man because of Joy. Because she had brought him back to life. Awakened him after too many years spent in a self-made prison.

"So what the hell are you going to do about it?" he muttered, hating the way his voice echoed in the vast room. He picked up his beer, took a long drink and glared at the glittering Christmas tree. The night they'd decorated it flooded his mind.

Holly laughing, a fresh row of stitches on her forehead to remind him just how fear for her had brought him to his knees. Joy standing back and telling him where lights were missing. The three of them eating more candy canes than they hung and finally, Holly falling asleep, not knowing that he was going to screw everything up.

He pushed up out of the chair, walked to the tree and looked beyond it, to the lights in the fairy houses outside. There were pieces of both of them all over this place, he thought. There was no escaping the memories this time, even if he wanted to.

Turning, he looked around the room and felt the solitude press in on him. The immense room felt claustrophobic. Joy should be here with him, drinking wine and eating "winter" cookies. Holly should be calling for a drink of water and trying to stay up a little later.

"Instead," he muttered, like the hermit he was, "you're alone with your memories."

Joy was right, he told himself. Fate had cheated him once, stealing away those he loved best. But he'd done it to himself this time. He'd taken his second chance and thrown it away because he was too afraid to grab on and never let go. He thought about all he'd lost—all he was about to lose—and had to ask himself if pain was really all he had. Was that what he'd become? A man devoted to keeping his misery alive and well no matter the cost?

He put his beer down, stalked out of the room and headed for the workshop. "Damned if it is."

Christmas morning dawned with a soft snow falling, turning the world outside the tiny house in Franklin into a postcard.

The small, bent-over tree stood on a table in the living room, and even the multiple strings of lights it boasted couldn't make it a quarter as majestic as the tree they'd left behind in Sam's great room. But this one, Joy assured herself, was *theirs*. Hers and Holly's. And that made it perfect. They didn't need the big tree. Or the lovely house. Or Sam. They had each other and that was enough.

It just didn't *feel* like enough anymore. Giving herself a mental kick for even thinking those words, Joy pushed thoughts of Sam out of her mind. No small task since the last four or five days had been a study in loneliness. Holly was sad, Joy was miserable, and even the approach of Christmas hadn't been enough to lift the pall that hung over them both.

Deb had tried to cheer her, telling her that everything happened for a reason, but really? When the reason was a stubborn, foolish man too blind to see what he was giving up, what comfort was there?

Ignoring the cold hard stone settled around her heart, Joy forced a smile and asked, "Do you want to go outside, sweetie? Try out your new sled?"

Holly sat amid a sea of torn wrapping paper, its festive colors and bold ribbons making it look as though the presents had exploded rather than been opened. Her blond hair was loose, and her pink princess nightgown was tucked up around her knees as she sat cross-legged in the middle of the rubble.

She turned big blue eyes on Joy and said, "No, Mommy, I don't want to right now."

"Really?" Joy was trying to make Christmas good for her daughter, but the little girl missed Sam as much as Joy did, so it was an uphill battle. But they had to get used to being without him, didn't they? He'd made his choice. He'd let them go, and she hadn't heard a word from him since.

Apparently Sam Henry had found a way to go on,

and so would she and Holly. "Well, how about we watch your favorite princess movie and drink some hot chocolate?"

"Okay…" The lack of enthusiasm in that word told Joy that Holly was only agreeing to please her mother.

God, she was a terrible person. *She's* the one who had allowed Holly to get too close to Sam in the hopes of reaching him. She had seen her daughter falling in love and hadn't done enough to stop it. She'd been too caught up in the sweetness of Holly choosing her own father to prepare either of them for the time when it all came crashing down on them.

Still, she had to try to reach her baby girl. Ease the pain, help her to enjoy Christmas morning.

"Are you upset because Santa couldn't bring you the puppy you wanted? Santa left you the note," Joy said, mentally thanking Sam for at least coming up with that brilliant idea. "He'll bring you a puppy as soon as he's old enough."

"It's okay. I can play with Lizzie's puppy." Holly got up, walked to her mother and crawled into her lap. Leaning her head against Joy's chest, she sighed heavily. "I want to go see Sam."

Joy's heart gave one hard lurch as everything in her yearned for the same thing. "Oh, honey, I don't think that's a good idea."

"Sure it is." Holly turned in her lap, looked up into her eyes and said softly, "He misses me, Mommy.

It's Christmas and he's all by himself and lonely and probably crabby some more cuz we're not there to make him smile and help him with the fairy houses. He *needs* us. And we belong with Sam. It's Christmas and we should be there."

Her baby girl looked so calm, so serious, so *sure* of everything. The last few days hadn't been easy. They'd slipped back into their old life, but it wasn't the same. Nothing was the same anymore. They were a family as they'd always been, but now it felt as if someone was missing.

She'd left Sam to protect Holly. But keeping her away from the man she considered her father wasn't helping her either. It was a fine line to walk, Joy knew. She smoothed Holly's hair back from her face and realized her baby girl was right.

Sam had let them leave, but it was Joy who had packed up and walked out. Neither of them had fought for what they wanted, so maybe it was time to make a stand. Time to let him know that he could try to toss them aside all he wanted—but they weren't going to go.

"You're right, baby, he *does* need us. And we need him." Giving Holly a quick, hard kiss, she grinned and said, "Let's get dressed."

Sam heard the car pull into the drive, looked out the window and felt his heart jump to life. How was *that* for timing? He'd just been getting into his coat to drive into Franklin and bring his girls home. He felt like Ebenezer Scrooge when he woke up on Christmas morning and realized he hadn't missed it. Hadn't lost his last chance at happiness.

He hit the front door at a dead run and made it to the car before Joy had turned off the engine. Snow was falling, he was freezing, but he didn't give a good damn. Suddenly everything in his world had righted itself. And this time, he was going to grab hold of what was most important and never let it go again.

"Sam! Sam! Hi, Sam!" Holly's voice, hitting that high note, sounded like the sweetest song to him.

"Hi, Holly!" he called back, and while the little girl got herself out of her seat belt, he threw open the driver's door and pulled Joy out. "Hi," he said, letting his gaze sweep over her features before focusing back on the eyes that had haunted him from the first moment they met.

"Hi, Sam. Merry Christmas." She cupped his cheek in her palm, and her touch melted away the last of the ice encasing his heart.

"I missed you, damn it," he muttered and bent to kiss her. That first taste of her settled everything inside him, brought the world back into focus and let him know that he was alive. And grateful.

"We're back!" Holly raced around the car, threw herself at Sam's legs and held on.

Breaking the kiss, he grinned down at the little girl and then reached down to pick her up. Holding her tight, he looked into bright eyes and then spun her in circles until she squealed in delight. "You're back. Merry Christmas, Holly."

She hugged his neck tightly and kissed his cheek with all the ferocity of a five-year-old's love. "Merry Christmas!"

"Come on, you two. It's cold out here." He carried Holly and followed behind Joy as she walked into the house and then turned for the great room. "I've got a couple surprises for you two."

"For Christmas?" Holly gave him a squeeze, then as she saw what was waiting for her, breathed, "Oh my goodness!" That quick gasp was followed by another squeal, this one higher than the one before. She squirmed to get out of Sam's arms, then raced across the room to the oversize fairy castle dollhouse sitting in front of the tree.

Beside him, Sam heard Joy give a soft sigh. When he looked at her, there were tears in her eyes and a beautiful smile on her amazing mouth. His heart gave another hard lurch, and he welcomed it. For the last few days, he'd felt dead inside. Coming back to life was much better.

"You made that for her."

He looked to where the girl he already considered his daughter was exploring the castle he'd built for her. It was red, with turrets and towers, tiny flags flying from the points of those towers. Glass windows opened and closed, and wide double doors swung open. The back of the castle was open for small fingers to explore and redecorate and dream.

"Yeah," he said. "Holly needed a fairy house she could actually play with. I'm thinking this summer we might need to build a tree house, too."

"This summer?" Joy's words were soft, the question hanging in the air between them.

"I've got plans," he said. "And so much to tell you. Ask you."

Her eyes went soft and dreamy and as he watched, they filled with a sheen of tears he really hoped she wouldn't let fall.

"I can't believe you made that for Holly," Joy said, smiling at her daughter's excitement. "She loves it."

"I can't believe you're here," Sam confessed, turning her in his arms so he could hold her, touch her, look into her eyes. Sliding his hands up her arms, over her shoulders to her face, his palms cradled her as his thumbs stroked gently over her soft, smooth skin. "I was coming to you."

"You were?" Wonder, hope lit her eyes, and Sam knew he hadn't blown it entirely. He hadn't let this last best chance at love slip past him.

"You arrived just as I was headed to the garage. I was going to bring you back here to give you your presents. Here. In our home."

Her breath caught and she lifted one hand to her mouth. "*Our* home?"

"If you'll stay," he said. "Stay with me. Love me. Marry me."

"Oh, Sam…"

"Don't answer yet," he said, grinning now as he took her hand and pulled her over to the brightly lit Christmas tree. "Just wait. There's more." Then to the little girl, he said, "There's another present for you, Holly. I think Santa stopped off here last night."

"He *did*?" Holly's eyes went wide as saucers as her smile danced in her eyes. "What did he bring?"

"Open it and find out," he said and pointed to a big white box with a red ribbon.

"How come it has holes in the top?" Holly asked.

"You'll see."

Joy already guessed it. She squeezed Sam's hand as they watched Holly carefully lift off the lid of the box and peer inside. "Oh my goodness!"

The little girl looked up at Sam. "He's for me?"

"She is. It's a girl."

Holly laughed in delight then reached into the box and lifted out a golden retriever puppy. Its fur was white and soft, and Holly buried her face against that softness, whispering and laughing as the puppy eagerly licked her face. "Elsa. I'm gonna name her Elsa," Holly proclaimed and laid out on the floor so her new best friend could jump all over her in wild abandon.

"I can't believe you did that," Joy said, shaking her

head and smiling through her tears. "Where did you find a white puppy? I looked everywhere."

Sam shrugged and gave her a half smile. "My sister knew a breeder and, well… I chartered a jet and flew out to Boston to pick her up two days ago."

"Boston." Joy blinked at him. "You flew to Boston to pick up a Christmas puppy so my little girl wouldn't be disappointed."

"*Our* little girl," he corrected. "I love her, Joy. Like she's my own. And if you'll let me, I'll adopt her."

"Oh my God…" Joy bit down hard on her bottom lip and gave up the battle to stem her tears. They coursed down her cheeks in silvery rivers that only made her smile shine more brightly.

"Is that a yes?"

"Yes, of course it's a yes," Joy managed to say when she threw her arms around him and held on. "She already considers you her father. So do I."

Sam held Joy tight, buried his face in the curve of her neck and said, "I love you. Both of you. So much. I won't ever let you go, Joy. I want you to marry me. Give me Holly. And give us both more children. Help me make a family so strong nothing can ever tear it down."

"You filled my heart, Sam." She pulled back, looked up at him and said, "All of this. What you've done. It's the most amazing moment of my life. My personal crabby hermit has become my hero."

His mouth quirked at the corner. "Still not done," he said and drew her to the other side of the tree.

"You've already given me everything, Sam. What's left?" She was laughing and crying and the combined sounds were like music to him.

The big house felt full of love and promise, and Sam knew that it would never be empty again. There would be so much light and love in the house, shadows would be banished. He had his memories of lost love, and those would never fade, but he wouldn't be ruled by them anymore, either.

When Kaye finally came home from her annual vacation, she was going to find a changed man and a household that was filled with the kind of happiness Sam had thought he'd never find again.

"What is it, Sam?" Joy asked when he pulled her to a stop in front of a draped easel.

"A promise," he said and pulled the sheet from the painting he'd only just finished the night before, to show her what he dreamed. What he wanted. For both of them.

"Oh, Sam." Her heart was in her voice. He heard it and smiled.

Joy stared at the painting, unable to tear her eyes from it. He'd painted this room, with the giant, lit-up tree, with stacks of presents at its feet, and the hint of fairy lights from the tiny houses in the woods shining through the glass behind it.

On the floor, he'd painted Holly, the puppy climbing all over her as the little girl laughed. He'd painted him and Joy, arms around each other, watching the magic unfold together. And he'd painted Joy pregnant.

There was love and celebration in every stroke of paint. The light was warm and soft and seemed to make the painting glow with everything she was feeling. She took it all in and felt the wonder of it all settle in the center of her heart. He'd painted her a promise.

"I did it all yesterday," he said, snaking both arms around her middle as they stared at his creation. "I've never had a painting come so quickly. And I know it's because this is what's meant to be. You, me, Holly."

"I love it," Joy said softly, turning her face up just enough to meet his kiss. "But we don't know if I'm pregnant."

"If you're not now," he promised, both eyebrows lifting into high arches, "you will be soon. I want lots of kids with you, Joy. I want to live again—risks and all—and I can only do that if you love me."

She turned around in his arms, glanced at her daughter, still giggling with puppy delight, then smiled up at Sam. "I love you so much, Sam. I always will. I want to make that family with you. Have lots of kids. Watch Holly and the others we'll make together grow up with a father who loves them."

"We can do that. Hell," he said, "we can do anything together."

She took a long, deep breath and grinned up at him. "And if you ask me to marry you right this minute, this will be the best Christmas ever."

He dipped into his pocket, pulled out a sapphire and diamond ring and slid it onto her finger while she watched, stunned. Though she'd been hoping for a real proposal, she hadn't expected a ring. Especially one this beautiful.

"It wasn't just a puppy I got in Boston," he said. "Though I will admit my sister helped me pick out this ring."

"Your family knows?"

"Absolutely," he said, bending to kiss her, then kiss the ring on her finger as if sealing it onto her hand. "My mother's thrilled to have a granddaughter and can't wait to meet you both in person. And be prepared, they'll all be descending after the holidays to do just that."

"It'll be fun," she said. "Oh, Sam, I love *you*."

"That's the only present I'm ever going to need," Sam said and kissed her hard and long and deep.

She'd come here this morning believing she would have to fight with Sam to make him admit how much he loved her. The fact that he had been on his way to get her and Holly filled her heart. He wanted her. He loved them both. And he was willing to finally leave the past behind and build a future with her. It really was the best Christmas she'd ever known.

"Hey!" Holly tugged at both of them as the puppy jumped at her feet. "You're kissing! Like mommies and daddies do!"

Joy looked at her little girl as Sam lifted her up to eye level. "Would you like that, baby girl? Would you like Sam to be your daddy and for all of us to live here forever?"

"For really?"

"For really," Sam said. "I'd like to be your daddy, Holly. And this summer, you and I are going to build you a fairy tree house. How does that sound?"

She gave him a wide, happy grin. "You'll be good at it, Sam. I can tell and I love you lots."

"I love you back, Holly. Always will." He kissed her forehead.

"Can I call you Daddy now?"

"I'd really like that," he said and Joy saw the raw emotion glittering in his eyes.

Their little girl clapped and grinned hugely before throwing her arms around both their necks. "This is the bestest Christmas ever. I got just what I wanted. A puppy. A fairy house. And my own daddy."

Sam looked into Joy's eyes and she felt his love, his pleasure in the moment, and she knew that none of them would ever be lonely again.

"Merry Christmas, Sam."

"Merry Christmas, Joy."

And in the lights of the tree, he sealed their new life with a kiss that had Holly applauding and sent the new puppy barking.

Everything, Joy thought, was *perfect*.

* * * * *

Pick up these other sexy, emotional reads about wealthy alpha heroes finding family from USA TODAY bestselling author Maureen Child!

THE BABY INHERITANCE
TRIPLE THE FUN
DOUBLE THE TROUBLE
THE COWBOY'S PRIDE AND JOY
HAVE BABY, NEED BILLIONAIRE

Available now from Harlequin Desire!

***

If you're on Twitter, tell us what you think of Harlequin Desire! #harlequindesire

COMING NEXT MONTH FROM

HARLEQUIN *Desire*

Available January 3, 2017

#2491 THE TYCOON'S SECRET CHILD
Texas Cattleman's Club: Blackmail • by Maureen Child
When CEO Wesley Jackson's Twitter account is hacked, it's to reveal that he has a secret daughter! Amidst scandal, he tracks down his old fling, but can he convince her he's truly ready to be a father—and a husband?

#2492 ONE BABY, TWO SECRETS
Billionaires and Babies • by Barbara Dunlop
Wallflower Kate Dunhem goes undercover as a wild child to save her infant niece, but a torrid affair with a stranger who has his own secrets may turn her world upside down...

#2493 THE RANCHER'S NANNY BARGAIN
Callahan's Clan • by Sara Orwig
Millionaire Cade Callahan needs a nanny for his baby girl, but hiring his best friend's gorgeous, untouchable sister might have been a mistake! Especially once he can no longer deny the heat between them...

#2494 AN HEIR FOR THE TEXAN
Texas Extreme • by Kristi Gold
Years after a family feud ended their romance, wealthy rancher Austin reunites with his ex. Their chemistry is still just as explosive! But what will he do when he learns she's been withholding a serious secret?

#2495 SINGLE MOM, BILLIONAIRE BOSS
Billionaire Brothers Club • by Sheri WhiteFeather
Single mother Meagan Quinn has paid a price for her past mistakes, but when her sexy billionaire boss gives her a second chance, is she walking into a trap...or into a new life—with him?

#2496 THE BEST MAN'S BABY
by Karen Booth
She's the maid of honor. Her ex is the best man. Their friend's wedding must go off without a hitch—no fighting, no scandals, no hooking up! But after just one night, she's pregnant and the baby *might* be his...

YOU CAN FIND MORE INFORMATION ON UPCOMING HARLEQUIN® TITLES, FREE EXCERPTS AND MORE AT WWW.HARLEQUIN.COM.

HDCNM1216

SPECIAL EXCERPT FROM

H HARLEQUIN® *Desire*

*When CEO Wesley Jackson's Twitter account is hacked,
it's to reveal that he has a secret daughter! Amid
scandal, he tracks down his old fling, but can he convince
her he's truly ready to be a father—and a husband?*

Read on for a sneak peek at
THE TYCOON'S SECRET CHILD
by USA TODAY *bestselling author Maureen Child,
the first story in the new*
TEXAS CATTLEMAN'S CLUB: BLACKMAIL *series!*

"Look where your dallying has gotten you," the email
read.

"What the hell?" There was an attachment, and even
though Wes had a bad feeling about all of this, he opened
it. The photograph popped onto his computer screen.

Staring down at the screen, his gaze locked on the
image of the little girl staring back at him. "What the—"

She looked just like him.

Panic and fury tangled up inside him and tightened
into a knot that made him feel like he was choking.

A daughter? He had a child. Judging by the picture,
she looked to be four or five years old, so unless it was
an old photo, there was only one woman who could be
the girl's mother. And just like that, the woman was back,
front and center in his mind.

How the hell had this happened? Stupid. He knew how
it had happened. What he didn't know was why he hadn't

been told. Wes rubbed one hand along the back of his neck. Still staring at the smiling girl on the screen, he opened a new window and went to Twitter.

Somebody had hacked his account. His new account name was, as promised in the email, Deadbeatdad. If he didn't get this stopped fast, it would go viral and might start interfering with his business.

Instantly, Wes made some calls and turned the mess over to his IT guys to figure out. Meanwhile, he was too late to stop #Deadbeatdad from spreading. The Twitterverse was already moving on it. Now he had a child to find and a reputation to repair. Snatching up the phone, he stabbed the button for his assistant's desk. "Robin," he snapped. "Get Mike from PR in here now."

He didn't even wait to hear her response, just slammed the phone down and went back to his computer. He brought up the image of the little girl—his daughter—again and stared at her. What was her name? Where did she live?

Then thoughts of the woman who had to be the girl's mother settled into his brain. Isabelle Gray. She'd disappeared from his life years ago—apparently with his child.

Jaw tight, eyes narrowed, Wes promised himself he was going to get to the bottom of all of this.

Don't miss
THE TYCOON'S SECRET CHILD
by USA TODAY *bestselling author Maureen Child,*
available now wherever
Harlequin® Desire *books and ebooks are sold.*

www.Harlequin.com

Copyright © 2017 by Harlequin Books S.A.

HDEXP1216

Whatever You're Into… Passionate Reads

Looking for more passionate reads from Harlequin®?
Fear not! Harlequin® Presents, Harlequin® Desire and
Harlequin® Blaze offer you irresistible romance stories
featuring powerful heroes.

♦HARLEQUIN *Presents*

Do you want alpha males, decadent glamour and jet-set
lifestyles? Step into the sensational, sophisticated world of
Harlequin® Presents, where sinfully tempting heroes ignite a
fierce and wickedly irresistible passion!

♦HARLEQUIN *Desire*

Harlequin® Desire novels are powerful, passionate and
provocative contemporary romances set against a backdrop of
wealth, privilege and sweeping family saga. Alpha heroes with
a soft side meet strong-willed but vulnerable heroines amid a
dramatic world of divided loyalties, high-stakes conflict and
intense emotion.

♦HARLEQUIN *Blaze*

Harlequin® Blaze stories sizzle with strong heroines and
irresistible heroes playing the game of modern love and lust.
They're fun, sexy and always steamy.

Be sure to check out our full selection of books
within each series every month!

www.Harlequin.com

HPASSION2016

Turn your love of reading into
rewards you'll love with

Harlequin My Rewards

**Join for FREE today at
www.HarlequinMyRewards.com**

Earn **FREE BOOKS** of your choice.

Experience **EXCLUSIVE OFFERS** and contests.

Enjoy **BOOK RECOMMENDATIONS**
selected just for you.

PLUS! Sign up now
and get **500** points
right away!

Earn
FREE
REWARDS
HarlequinMyRewards.com
Join!
Today!

MYR16R